Dirty Bertie

A COLLECTION of CHAOS

DAVID ROBERTS WRITTEN BY ALAN MACDONALD

LITTLE TIGER

LONDON

Collect all the
Dirty Bertie books!

Worms!

Fleas!

Pants!

Burp!

Yuck!

Crackers!

Bogeys!

Mud!

Germs!

Loo!

Fetch!

Fangs!

Kiss!

Ouch!

Snow!

Pong!

Pirate!

Scream!

Toothy!

Dinosaur!

Zombie!

Smash!

Rats!

Horror!

Jackpot!

Aliens!

Fame!

Monster!

Disco!

Mascot!

Spider!

Trouble!

Bees!

Poop!

Contents

1   Worms!   5

2   Fetch!   99

3   Trouble!   193

STRIPES PUBLISHING LIMITED
An imprint of the Little Tiger Group
1 Coda Studios, 189 Munster Road,
London SW6 6AW

Imported into the EEA by Penguin Random House Ireland,
Morrison Chambers, 32 Nassau Street, Dublin D02 YH68

A paperback original
First published in Great Britain in 2022

Characters created by David Roberts
Text copyright © Alan MacDonald
Worms! 2006 • Fetch! 2010 • Trouble! 2020
Illustration copyright © David Roberts
Worms! 2006 • Fetch! 2010 • Trouble! 2020

ISBN: 978-1-78895-426-6

The Forest Stewardship Council® (FSC®) is a global, not-for-profit organization dedicated to
the promotion of responsible forest management worldwide. FSC® defines standards based
on agreed principles for responsible forest stewardship that are supported by environmental,
social, and economic stakeholders. To learn more, visit www.fsc.org

10 9 8 7 6 5 4 3 2 1

For Christine ~ D R

To the lovely Hylands of Hyland Hall ~ A M

Contents

1   Worms!   8

2   Manners!   42

3   Rubbish!   72

WORMS!

CHAPTER 1

It was Monday morning and Bertie was eating his breakfast.

"Bertie, don't do that!" said his mum, looking up.

"Do what?" said Bertie.

"Let Whiffer lick your spoon. I saw you!"

"He's hungry!" said Bertie.

Dirty Bertie

"I don't care," sighed Mum. "It's dirty, Bertie."

Bertie inspected his spoon and gave it a lick. It looked clean enough to him.

Just then he heard the post thudding through the letterbox. He jumped down from the table and skidded into the hall. Bertie hardly ever got a letter, but it didn't stop him checking the post. He sorted through the bundle. Dad, Mum, Mum, Dad, boring, boring ... wait!

A letter with his name written on it in large wonky letters!

To Bertie

Dirty Bertie

Bertie burst into the kitchen. "I got a letter!" He tore the envelope open. The decorations on the card could only mean one thing. A party!

Bertie loved birthday parties – he loved the games, the cake and the party bags. Last year he'd had a dog party and everyone had come as a dog. Bertie had been a bloodhound with Dracula fangs. He had wanted dog biscuits for tea but his mum had put her foot down.

Mum picked up the invitation. "Oh lovely, Bertie! Angela's invited you to her party."

"Angela?" said Bertie. The smile drained from his face. "Not Angela Angela?"

"Yes. Angela next door."

"Bertie's little girlfriend!" teased his sister, Suzy.

Bertie grabbed the invitation and read the message inside.

please come to my pink
Birthday party on Friday!
wear something pink!
Love and kisses
from Angela ×××

Bertie's mouth gaped open. His whole body drooped with disappointment. Angela Nicely lived next door and was almost six. She had straight blonde hair, rosy cheeks and large blue eyes. Worst of all she was in love with Bertie. She followed him round like a shadow.

Dirty Bertie

He didn't want to go to Angela's party, and he definitely didn't want to go to any party where you had to dress in pink. Bertie's favourite colour was brown. Mud was brown, fingernails were brown, poo was brown. Ribbons, bows and ballet shoes, they were pink.

"I don't have to go, do I?" asked Bertie.

"Nose, Bertie," said Mum.

Bertie removed a finger that had strayed up his nose.

"Angela's invited you," said Mum. "How would you feel if you invited Angela and she didn't come?"

"I'd feel glad," said Bertie, truthfully.

"It's a party, Bertie. You love parties," said Mum.

"And you love Angela!" taunted Suzy.

Dirty Bertie

Bertie ignored her. "It'll be terrible. They'll all want to play princesses. Couldn't you say I've got to go to the dentist?"

Mum gave him a look. "That would be a lie, wouldn't it, Bertie?"

"Mum! They'll all be girls," moaned Bertie. "I'll be the only boy!"

"I'm sure it'll be fun. Now, I'm late for work." She kissed him and hurried out. Bertie slumped into a chair.

A pink party with adoring Angela and her friends – could anything be worse?

CHAPTER 2

The next day Bertie overheard Mrs Nicely talking to his mum about the party. It was just as he feared. He was the only boy invited – along with six of Angela's friends. "Angela is so excited about Bertie coming," said Mrs Nicely. "I think it's so sweet she's invited her little boyfriend."

Dirty Bertie

Bertie was nearly sick. Boyfriend? Yuck! He wasn't Angela's boyfriend! If his friends ever heard about the party they'd make fun of him for weeks. He wasn't going and that was final. If his mum wouldn't think of an excuse then he'd have to invent one himself. When it came to cunning plans, Bertie was a master.

In his room he searched under the bed for the shoebox where he kept his top-secret possessions.

Dirty Bertie

He pulled out a notebook and began
to write a list:

Brilliant excuses ·for· not going
to a party.

1. A crocodile bit my head off
and I'm not talking to anyone.

2. I have got a rare disease
called party-itis which brings
me out in terrible spots.

3. I had baked beans for breakfast,
lunch and supper. I think you know
what that means.

4. I have lost my memory.

What party?

Dirty Bertie

Bertie read back through it. "Brilliant Excuse Number 4" would do the trick. Now all he had to do was talk to Angela and convince her. Then he would be off the hook. No stinky-pinky party for him.

Bertie's chance came on Wednesday lunchtime. He was eating lunch with his friends Darren and Eugene. They were flicking peas at the next table to see if they could land one down the back of Know-All Nick's jumper.

"Hello, Bertie!" said Angela, appearing from nowhere.

Bertie looked at her blankly. "Who are you?" he asked.

Angela giggled. "You are funny, Bertie! Did you get the invitation? You are coming to my party, aren't you?''

Bertie frowned. "Party? What party?''

"Silly! You know, my pink party!''

"PINK Party? Ha ha!'' hooted Darren. "Bertie's going to a GIRL'S party!''

Bertie shot him a look. "Sorry, I don't remember any party,'' he told Angela. "I've lost my memory, you see.''

"Gosh!'' said Angela. "How?''

"That's just it, I can't remember. I must have got a bang on the head.''

"Oh, poor Bertie!'' cooed Angela.

Eugene and Darren exchanged glances. "Poor Bertie!'' they mimicked.

Angela put her hand on Bertie's. Bertie drew it away quickly.

"Never mind,'' she said. "The party's at my house on Friday. We're having a bouncy castle.''

Dirty Bertie

"Have a nice time," said Bertie, loading more peas on to his spoon.

Angela stamped her foot.

"You've got to come, Bertie. Laura and Maisie are coming. I've told them you're my boyfriend."

Dirty Bertie

Eugene gurgled and slipped off his chair. Bertie stared hard at Angela as if she looked faintly familiar. "Sorry? What did you say your name was?"

Angela gave a howl of rage and stormed off. Bertie heaved a sigh of relief. It had been a close call but he thought he'd got away with it.

Later that evening Mrs Nicely called to see his mum. Sensing trouble, Bertie hid in his room. But as soon as the front door closed, there was a shout from downstairs.

"BERTIE! Down here! Now!"

Bertie slunk downstairs.

"Right," said Mum. "What's this about losing your memory?"

Bertie stared at his feet. "Um … yes. It just seems to keep um … going."

"Really? So you don't remember Angela's invitation?"

Bertie knit his brows. "What invitation?" he asked.

Mum folded her arms. "That's a pity, because there's a film you wanted to see at the weekend. I expect you've forgotten that too?"

Bertie hadn't. "Pirates of Blood Island!" he blurted out. He'd been begging to see the film for weeks.

"Ah! So your memory is working," said Mum.

"I … um … remember some things. But other things I forget."

"Hmm," said Mum. "Well don't worry because I've marked the party on the

calendar to remind you." She pointed
to Friday the 8th — it was ringed in red.
"And Bertie…"

"Yes?"

"I will not forget."

Bertie slunk out of the kitchen.

He knew when he was beaten.

CHAPTER 3

Thursday sped by. Friday came. After school Bertie played in his room with his pet earthworm, Arthur. Bertie kept him in a goldfish bowl filled with mud, leaves and a plastic soldier for company. He was trying to train Arthur to come when he called him. "Arthur! Arthur!" he coaxed.

Dirty Bertie

"Bertie!" called Mum from downstairs.

"Just a minute!" shouted Bertie. He hid the bowl under the bed. His mum didn't exactly know about Arthur yet. A moment later she poked her head round the door.

"Come on, Bertie! You'll be late for the party."

"What party?"

"That's not going to work," said Mum.

"But … but … I haven't got a present," said Bertie, desperately.

Mum held up two boxes. "The doll or the face paints?" she said.

"Face paints," said Bertie, gloomily. He wasn't going to turn up holding a doll.

"Oh, and I bought you this to wear." Mum handed him a brand new T-shirt.

"Blech!" said Bertie. "It's pink. I can't wear that!"

Dirty Bertie

"Don't be silly, Bertie, it's a pink party. Now hurry up and get ready." She disappeared, leaving him with the pink horror.

Bertie retrieved Arthur from under the bed. He held the T-shirt against him and looked in the mirror.

"What do you think, Arthur?" he asked. "Yucky or what?"

Dirty Bertie

Suddenly Bertie had the most brilliant brainwave. The invitation said to wear something pink. Well, worms were pink, weren't they? He could go to the party as an earthworm! All he needed was something pink and wormy to wear.

Bertie tiptoed into his parents' room. Strictly speaking he wasn't allowed in there, not since he'd used Mum's favourite perfume to make a stinkbomb.

Opening the wardrobe, he began to pull out armfuls of clothes. Nothing pink there. But then – bingo! – on top of the wardrobe he spotted something. Suzy's sleeping bag, the one she was taking to school camp. It was bright pink with a hood that fitted snugly over your head – perfect for an earthworm. All it needed was the finishing touch.

Dirty Bertie

Ten minutes later Bertie's mum found him in the back garden.

"Oh, Bertie! No, Bertie!" she wailed.

"What?" said Bertie.

"You're filthy. Look at you!"

Bertie scrambled to his feet and inspected his costume. He was impressively dirty – but that was the whole point of rolling in a flowerbed.

Dirty Bertie

"Earthworms are meant to be muddy," he explained. "They live underground."

"Bertie! I asked you to get ready for the party!"

"I am. It said to go in pink, so I am. I'm going as an earthworm."

Mum looked closer. "What is that?" she said. "It's not Suzy's sleeping bag?"

"It is!" beamed Bertie. "It's perfect!"

The sleeping bag was smeared with mud. It covered Bertie from head to toe with only his grimy face peeping out. Mum sat down heavily on the rockery.

"Bertie, you can't go like that."

"Why not?" said Bertie. "It's pink. I bet no one else'll be going as an earthworm."

"No," sighed Mum, wearily. "I doubt if they will."

CHAPTER 4

Angela's front door was festooned with pink balloons. Mum walked up the path with Bertie hopping after her like a giant pink jumping bean and rang the doorbell. Mrs Nicely came to the door.

"Hello!" she said and then, "Oh good heavens!" as her eye fell on Bertie.

"I'm an earthworm," Bertie explained.

Dirty Bertie

"How … ah … lovely, Bertie," said Mrs Nicely. "Do come in."

Bertie showered clods of earth on to the carpet as he bounced into the hall.

Most of Angela's friends had come as princesses and fairies. The front room was a sea of pink tutus.

"You're here, Bertie!" said Angela, running up to him. "I'm a fairy. Look, I've got wings!"

"I'm an earthworm," said Bertie. "I got you a present."

An arm emerged from the sleeping bag holding a scruffy package. Angela tore off the wrapping paper. "Thank you!" she trilled, dropping the face paints on top of her big pile of presents. Bertie gazed at them longingly.

"Let's play a game," said Mrs Nicely.

Dirty Bertie

"Who wants to play Musical Statues?"

"Me! Me!" chorused the fairies and princesses.

The music played and they all danced round the room.

"Bertie isn't dancing!" moaned Angela.

"Yes I am," said Bertie. "This is how earthworms dance!"

Bertie rolled over and over on the floor so that the dancing fairies had to jump over him. The music suddenly stopped.

Dirty Bertie

"Statues everybody! Statues!" cried
Mrs Nicely. The fairies and princesses
became wobbling statues. But Bertie,
who was feeling a little hot and dizzy,
hadn't been listening. He just kept rolling
… straight into one of the fairies.

Laura wobbled and fell into Angela…
Angela wobbled and fell on top of
Maisie and Clare…

Soon all the statues had collapsed in
a heap. Bertie rolled to a halt at Mrs
Nicely's feet. "Did I win?" he asked.

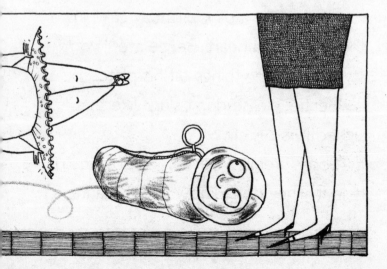

Dirty Bertie

Tea was pink. Pink biscuits, pink
ice cream and a pink birthday cake in
the shape of a heart. Bertie ate "worm-
style" by licking things off his plate.

"Bertie, please don't slurp like that,"
sighed Mrs Nicely.

"Sorry," replied Bertie. "Worms can't
help it. They don't know about manners."

Dirty Bertie

When tea was over Mrs Nicely
surveyed the mess on the floor. Most of
it had collected under Bertie's chair.

"Can we go on the bouncy castle
now?" asked Bertie, tugging at her sleeve.

"In a minute, Bertie!" she said.
"Angela, why don't you all go next door
and play with your presents?"

While Angela's friends played with her
Little Patty Pony set, Bertie eyed the face
paints. Maybe he would just try one? He
wriggled an arm out of his sleeping bag
and selected a black face paint. He drew
on his chin and looked in the mirror.
Next he drew on his cheeks. Perhaps he
would turn himself into a vampire or a
zombie? Or better still…

He was so busy that he didn't notice
the room had gone quiet.

Dirty Bertie

Dirty Bertie

"Oh Bertie!" said Angela.

"Ah," said Bertie, "I was just … um … borrowing them."

"What have you done to your face?"

"I'm a slug," said Bertie.

"You said you were a worm."

"I was, but now I'm a slug. A big black, slimy slug."

He slithered on to the floor, making slimy, sluggy noises. Angela's friends shrieked with delight and ran to hide behind the curtains. Angela peeped out, her eyes shining. "Make me a slug too, Bertie," she pleaded.

Mrs Nicely was still tidying up when the doorbell rang. Thank goodness it was over for another year. She went to answer the door. Bertie's mum stood on the doorstep with three other parents.

"I do hope Bertie's behaved himself," she said.

"Oh yes," said Mrs Nicely. "He's such a … lively boy." She led them through to the back door. "They're all playing in the garden," she said. "Angela's had such a lovely time. They've all been good as…"

Mrs Nicely stopped in her tracks. Eight children were bouncing on the bouncy castle. But the princesses and fairies who had come to the party had vanished. In their place were ugly green monsters in filthy tutus who looked like they'd crawled from a swamp.

In the middle of them all was Bertie, bouncing and whooping.

Dirty Bertie

"Look, Mum!" sang Angela. "I'm a creepy caterpillar! Bertie did it!"

Mrs Nicely looked at Bertie's mum. The other parents looked at Bertie's mum. Bertie's mum looked at Bertie.

"What?" said Bertie.

Back in his room, Bertie was glad to be reunited with Arthur. Personally he couldn't see why everyone had made such a fuss. What was the point of giving someone face paints if they weren't allowed to use them?

"Anyway," he told Arthur with a smile. "I don't think they'll be inviting me next year."

He considered it. Really the party hadn't turned out so badly.

Dirty Bertie

He felt in his pocket and brought out something pink and sticky.

"Look, Arthur!" he said. "I saved you some cake!"

MANNERS!

CHAPTER 1

Bertie had no manners. His family all agreed. He lolled, he fidgeted and talked with his mouth full. He sniffed and slurped and burped and picked his nose.

"Bertie, use a hanky!"

"Take your elbows off the table!"

"Don't touch that, it's dirty, Bertie!" his parents moaned every day.

Dirty Bertie

Bertie didn't see the point. Animals didn't make all this fuss. Did pigs or dogs have manners? When Whiffer weed against a tree no one seemed to mind. Yet if Bertie had done that his mum would have fainted on the spot.

No, in Bertie's opinion manners were a waste of time. But that was before he heard about the prize.

It was the head teacher, Miss Skinner, who had announced the prize in assembly one morning.

"Does anyone know what tomorrow is?" she asked. Her gaze fell on Bertie who was crossing his eyes at Darren.

"Bertie!" she said.

"Uh … yes, Miss?"

Dirty Bertie

"Do you know what tomorrow is?"
Bertie thought. "Tuesday?" he said.

Miss Skinner gave him one of her
looks. "Tomorrow," she said, "is National
Courtesy Day. It's a day when we should
be especially polite, so I want us all to
think about our manners. We are lucky
to have Miss Prim from the library
coming to visit us, and she has agreed to
present a very special prize to the child
with the best manners."

"Huh! Special prize!" said Bertie to
Darren as they trooped back to the
classroom. "I bet it's some boring old
book about being polite."

"Actually it's not," said a reedy voice
behind them. It was Know-All Nick,
Bertie's worst enemy.

"How do you know?" asked Bertie.

"Because I heard Miss Skinner tell Miss Boot," said Nick, looking pleased with himself. "She said the tickets had come this morning."

"Tickets for what?" asked Darren.

"Wouldn't you like to know!" sneered Nick (who would have liked to know himself).

"I bet it's football tickets!" said Darren.

"Or cinema tickets," said Donna.

"Or tickets for Mega Mayhem," said Bertie, his eyes lighting up. Mega Mayhem was the best theme park in the world and he'd been begging to go for months.

"It doesn't matter what it is," said Nick, smugly. "I'm bound to win. My mum says I've got beautiful manners."

"It's a pity your face is so ugly," muttered Bertie.

Dirty Bertie

Bertie thought about the prize for the rest of the day. He was sure the tickets were for Mega Mayhem and he'd made up his mind to win them. Even if it meant he had to be polite for a whole day he didn't care. After all, how hard could it be?

CHAPTER 2

The next morning Bertie bounded out of bed. Today was National Courtesy Day – the day he was going to win the prize. On the landing he met his mum returning from the bathroom.

"Good morning, Mum," he said. "Isn't it a lovely morning?"

His mum gave him a suspicious look.

Dirty Bertie

"What have you done, Bertie?"

"I haven't done anything," said Bertie. "I was just being polite."

Downstairs Dad and Suzy were eating breakfast.

"Good morning!" Bertie greeted them cheerfully, as he sat down.

He poured Frostie Flakes into his bowl and cleared his throat. "Ahem. Would you pass the milk please, Suzy?"

Suzy stared at him. "Why are you talking in that funny way?"

"It's not a funny way, thank you. It's called being polite."

Bertie poured milk into his bowl without spilling a drop and sucked his Frostie Flakes so as not to make a noise. Even when he dropped his spoon he was careful to wipe it on his jumper before putting it in his mouth.

"I might be getting a prize today," he announced.

Dad looked up. "Mmm? What kind of prize?"

"For being polite," said Bertie. "It's National Courtesy Day and they're giving a prize for being polite."

"You? Polite? HA!" snorted Suzy.

Bertie sniffed. "I'm more polite than you, fat-face."

"Nose, Bertie," said Dad. "Where's your hanky?"

Bertie pulled a grubby hanky from his pocket and wiped his nose. Something fell out and plopped into the sugar bowl.

Dirty Bertie

"Eugghh!" shrieked Suzy. "What's that?"

"It's only Buzz. He won't hurt you," said Bertie, picking out the large bluebottle.

"Bertie! It's a dead fly!" said Dad.

Dirty Bertie

"I know," replied Bertie. "Don't worry, I'm going to bury him."

Bertie had found Buzz lying on his window sill. He had decided to bury him under the apple tree. He blew off the sugar that was stuck to his wings.

"Put it away!" said Dad. "It's filthy!"

Bertie sighed and wrapped Buzz inside his hanky. He would bury him after school. That was the trouble he thought, you did your best to be polite and all you got was people shouting at you.

CHAPTER 3

Miss Prim stood at the front of the class. She was tall and thin. Her glasses hung round her neck on a cord. Bertie thought she must be a hundred at least. He'd seen Miss Prim at the library where she stood behind a desk and stamped people's books. He hoped she didn't remember him. Last time he'd been to the library Whiffer had done something in the story corner and they'd had to leave quickly.

"This is Miss Prim," said Miss Boot. "I hope we're all going to show her how well-mannered we can be." She ran her eye over her class, who were all sitting up straight and paying attention. It was marvellous the effect a prize could have. Even Bertie wasn't lolling in his seat or pushing a pencil up his nose.

Miss Prim talked to the class about the importance of good manners. Bertie tried to listen but his mind kept drifting off. He was imagining whizzing down the Slide of Doom at Mega Mayhem.

"Now," said Miss Boot. "Who would like to show our visitor around the school? Let's have two volunteers."

Dirty Bertie

Bertie's hand shot in the air. This was his chance to show Miss Prim how polite he could be. Unfortunately everyone else in his class had the same idea. Thirty children strained out of their seats waving their hands in the air. "Miss! Ooh, Miss! Please, Miss!"

Dirty Bertie

Miss Boot pointed. "Nick. I'm sure you'll look after our visitor."

Bertie couldn't believe it. Not Know-All Nick – why did he always get picked? Just because he'd made Miss Boot a soppy card on her birthday. It wasn't fair – Bertie never got picked for anything.

Miss Boot hesitated. She needed someone else who was polite and reliable.

"Miss, ooh, Miss! Me, Miss!"

"What about that boy at the back who's sitting so quietly?" suggested Miss Prim.

"Oh," said Miss Boot. "Not Bertie?"

Bertie, who hadn't been listening, looked up. "Me?" he said.

Dirty Bertie

Miss Prim walked down the corridor, admiring the paintings on the walls.

"That one's mine," said Nick, pointing to a bright picture of a sunset.

"And that one's mine," said Bertie, pointing to a splodgy mess of green. "It's an alien. And that's his dinner inside him."

"Ah," said Miss Prim. "How unusual. Don't we have a hanky, Bertie?"

"Oh yes. 'Scuse me," said Bertie. He pulled out his hanky and offered it to Miss Prim.

"No, I meant you. You need to wipe your nose!"

"Oh. Thanks," said Bertie. He wiped his nose on his sleeve and pocketed his hanky. He'd just remembered Buzz was wrapped inside and he didn't want him falling out.

Dirty Bertie

Miss Prim sighed heavily. "Perhaps we could look in the next class," she said.

Nick started to walk ahead quickly. Bertie kept pace with him. There was a mad dash for the door and they both grabbed the handle at once.

"I was first!"

"I was!"

"I was!"

Miss Prim caught up with them. "Boys, boys! I hope we're not squabbling," she said.

"Oh no," smiled Nick. "I was just telling Bertie his shirt's hanging out."

Bertie looked behind him. Nick wrenched open the door, squashing Bertie behind it.

Dirty Bertie

"After you, Miss," said Nick. Miss Prim
beamed at him.

"Thank you, Nicholas. It's nice to see
someone remembers their manners."

CHAPTER 4

By lunchtime Bertie was exhausted. Being polite was hard work, especially with Know-All Nick trying to outdo him the whole time. And now it looked as if he was stuck with Miss Prim for lunch.

As they crossed the hall, Bertie could hardly believe his eyes. No one in the dinner queue was pushing and shoving.

Dirty Bertie

There was no running or fighting or firing peas across the room. Everyone was eating their lunch quietly and politely.

"Hello, Miss Prim!" called Donna, as they passed by.

Bertie gulped. Three of his teachers were waiting for them at a table laid with a white tablecloth and a vase of flowers.

"Do come and join us," said Miss Skinner. "Bertie will fetch your lunch."

"Careful you don't drop it, Bertie!" whispered Know-All Nick.

"Careful I don't drop it on you," muttered Bertie.

Bertie sat opposite Miss Prim and Know-All Nick and stared at the plate in front of him. Spaghetti – how was he meant

Dirty Bertie

to eat that without making a mess? He watched Miss Prim wind spaghetti round her fork and tried to copy her. The spaghetti fell off before it reached his mouth. Nick put a hand over his mouth and loudly sucked up a piece of spaghetti. "Shloooooop!"

"Bertie!" he said. "Don't be so disgusting!"

Dirty Bertie

The teachers all looked in Bertie's direction.

"But ... it wasn't me!" gasped Bertie. "It was him!"

Miss Prim made a tutting noise. "Don't tell tales, Bertie, it isn't nice."

Bertie turned to glare at Nick. He would have liked to put spaghetti down his neck. He would have liked to pour a jug of water down his pants. But he wanted those tickets and Miss Prim was watching him like a hawk. As he lifted his fork to his mouth a hand jogged his elbow.

SPLAT! A splodge of sauce landed on the white tablecloth.

"Oh Bertie, you are messy!" jeered Nick. "Look what you've done!"

Miss Prim made another tutting noise.

"But it wasn't ME!" shouted Bertie.

Miss Boot glared.

Bertie ground his teeth. He would get that two-faced slimy sneak.

Nick was sent to fetch dessert.

Bertie's eyes lit up. Chocolate fudge cake – his favourite. He reached out to grab a piece.

"Manners, Bertie," Miss Prim reminded him. "We don't grab, we offer the plate to others."

Bertie reluctantly passed the cake round the table. Miss Skinner took a slice, so did Miss Boot and Mr Plumly. Bertie watched anxiously as the cake began to disappear.

"Oh dear," said Miss Prim, helping herself. "Only one piece left! Which of you is going to have it?"

Dirty Bertie

Bertie looked at Nick. Nick looked at Bertie. Both of them eyed the last slice of fudge cake. Then Nick did a surprising thing – he offered the plate to Bertie.

"You have it, Bertie," he said with a sickly smile. "I don't mind, really."

Bertie wasn't going to fall for that one. "That's okay, Nick, I want you to have it."

"Oh, well, if you insist," said Nick. "We don't want it going to waste." He snatched the last piece and took a large bite. "Thanks, Bertie."

Dirty Bertie

Bertie glared furiously. He'd been tricked! Well, that was it. No more manners, this was war. That fudge cake was his by right and he was going to get it back. Bertie reached into his pocket and brought out his hanky. Nick was too busy talking to Miss Prim to notice a hand dart across the table.

"Any second now," thought Bertie. "Five, four, three, two…"

Nick reached for the cake and raised it to his mouth. There was something black on top.

"ARGHHHHH! A fly!" screamed Nick, dropping the cake on the table.

"ARGGHHHH!" shrieked Miss Prim as Buzz landed in front of her.

"I'll get it!" cried Miss Skinner. She seized a spoon and attacked the bluebottle.

Dirty Bertie

SMACK! WHACK! THUMP! Plates and cups leaped in the air. Buzz hopped and jumped with each blow, showing surprising speed for a dead fly.

Miss Boot grabbed the water jug and emptied it over the table. SPLOOSH!

Buzz lay still in a puddle with his legs in the air.

"Is it dead?" asked Miss Skinner. She picked up the fly by one leg and examined it.

Dirty Bertie

The silence was broken by a loud burp.

Six pairs of eyes turned on Bertie. He had cake crumbs round his mouth and a satisfied smile on his face.

"Bertie!" said Miss Skinner.

"Um… Pardon me!" said Bertie, politely. He held out his hand. "Could I have my fly back, please?"

Dirty Bertie

Later that afternoon Bertie crowded into the hall with everyone else. The moment had arrived for Miss Prim to announce the winner of the prize. Bertie knew he didn't stand a chance – not after all the trouble at lunchtime. At least he'd been able to rescue Buzz from the litter bin. In any case it had all been worth it to see the look on Know-All Nick's face when he'd come eye to eye with Buzz. Bertie didn't mind who won the prize – as long as it wasn't Nick.

"And the winner," said Miss Prim, "is Nicholas Payne."

Bertie groaned. Know-All Nick made his way to the front and shook Miss Prim's hand. Everyone craned their necks to see what his prize would be. Miss Prim handed him an envelope. "As you're always so polite I'm sure you're going to love this. It's two tickets for the Museum of Manners in London."

Nick turned white. His mouth gaped open but nothing came out.

Bertie leaned forward. "Manners, Nick," he said. "Aren't you going to say thank you?"

CHAPTER 1

RUMBLE, RUMBLE! SCREECH! SNORT!

Something was making a noise outside Bertie's window. He sat up in bed. It was Saturday, Bertie's favourite day of the week. Saturday was bin day. He pulled back his curtains. Sure enough, there was the dustcart at the far end of the road. If he hurried he would be just in time.

Dirty Bertie

Downstairs he found Mum making tea in the kitchen.

"Morning, Bertie…" She broke off and stared at him. "What on earth are you wearing?"

Bertie looked at his outfit. He had on his dad's painting overalls, a woolly hat and a muddy pair of wellingtons. True, the overalls were a bit big, but Bertie thought they were perfect for a bin man.

Dirty Bertie

"It's Saturday," he said. "I've got to help Ed with the bins."

"Oh Bertie, not today," sighed Mum.

"Why not?"

"It's the summer fair this morning. I don't want you getting filthy."

"That's why I'm wearing these!" said Bertie, flapping his long sleeves.

"Anyway," said Mum, "you're too late. I took the rubbish out last night."

"But I always do it!" cried Bertie.

"Sorry, I forgot. You can do it next time."

He stared after his mum as she disappeared upstairs with her tea. Whiffer looked up from a bone he was licking and blinked at him. "How could she forget?" asked Bertie. "I always take the rubbish out on Saturdays!"

Dirty Bertie

When he grew up Bertie had decided he wanted to be a bin man. He wanted to wear an orange jacket and big gloves and ride in a truck that snorted like a dragon. Most of all he wanted to work with mountains of messy, smelly, sticky rubbish. Bertie loved rubbish. He had piles of it under his bed. String, lolly sticks, rubber bands, sweet wrappers – it was amazing what people threw away!

He began to rummage in the drawers. The bin men would be here any minute. Finally he found what he was looking for – a large black bin bag. All he needed now was a few bits of rubbish to fill it. Bertie looked around.

In went a dishcloth, a bar of soap, a tin of cat food and a pile of letters from Bertie's school (no one ever read them

anyway). In went his dad's slippers, some
carrots (yuck!), a cauliflower (double
yuck!) and his sister's pony magazine.

Rumble, rumble! The dustcart was
coming. Bertie scooted into the hall
dragging his bag behind him. Someone
had left a pot of old flowers by the front
door ready to throw out. Bertie
scooped it into the bag with the rest.

Dirty Bertie

The wheelie bin stood on the pavement. Bertie climbed on to the front wall so he could reach to drop his bag in. He peered into the bin, sniffing the sweet smell of rotting vegetables.

In one corner he caught sight of something familiar. Wasn't that his chewing gum collection? Surely his mum hadn't thrown it out? He bent into the bin to try and rescue it. The jar was just out of reach of his fingertips. He'd have to… "ARGHHH!" Bertie toppled in head first.

Dirty Bertie

His face was wedged against something soft and squashy. "Mmff! Help!"

"Hello, mate," said a voice. "Having a bit of trouble there?" Strong hands pulled him out and set him on his feet.

"Oh dear!" grinned Ed. "Your mum's going to be pleased."

Bertie inspected himself. He did seem to have got a bit messy. There was something sticky on his overalls that smelled like tomato ketchup. He brushed off some tea leaves and straightened his hat. A piece of potato peel fell off. He held up the rescued jam-jar to show Ed.

"I was looking for this. It's my chewing gum collection," he explained. "I'm doing an experiment to see what happens when it gets really old."

"And what does happen?" Ed asked.

Dirty Bertie

"It goes hard and it tastes really disgusting," said Bertie. "Want to try a bit?"

"No thanks," smiled Ed. "I've got to get on. Want to give me a hand?"

"Yes please!" said Bertie. "I brought you an extra bag today."

Bertie presented him with the rubbish he'd collected. Ed dropped the bag in the wheelie bin and Bertie pulled it to the waiting truck. He watched fascinated as the truck opened its metal jaws and swallowed up the rubbish. Ed held out a gloved hand and Bertie shook it.

"Good work, mate," said Ed. "See you next week." He moved off down the road, whistling.

"See you!" called Bertie.

CHAPTER 2

Back in the house, Bertie whistled as he spooned dog food into Whiffer's bowl. He whistled as he took off his overalls and sat down to have some breakfast.

"Bertie, please!" said Dad.

"What?" said Bertie. "I'm only whistling."

"That isn't whistling. You sound like you've got a puncture."

"Well I've got to practise," said Bertie. "How can I learn to whistle if you don't let me practise?"

Mum came into the kitchen looking flustered.

"Bertie, have you seen my flower arrangement? I left it by the front door this morning."

Bertie paused with his finger in the peanut butter. "By the door?"

Dirty Bertie

"Yes, it's for the competition at the summer fair. I spent hours working on it and now it's disappeared. Are you sure you haven't seen it?"

"Me? Um … no."

"Are you all right? You look a bit pale."

"I'm fine," said Bertie, who suddenly wasn't feeling so well. He remembered the pot of old flowers by the front door. He remembered putting it in his rubbish bag. Uh oh – the dustcart must have eaten it. Now he thought about it his mum had been going on about the competition for weeks. First prize always went to Mrs Nicely next door, but this year Bertie's mum felt she stood a chance. Or she would have done… How was Bertie to know the flowers by the door were hers? They looked practically dead!

Dirty Bertie

He got up from the table and sidled towards the door.

"Where are you going?" asked Mum. "You haven't finished your breakfast."

"I just need to do something."

"And what's this all over Dad's overalls?"

"Just ketchup. I had a bit of an accident."

"Bertie…!"

But Bertie was making for the door. If he was going to get those flowers back he would need to move fast.

CHAPTER 3

Bertie bent over the handlebars of his bike, pedalling at top speed. Whiffer scampered behind, trying to keep up. Maybe he was too late already. Even if he caught up with the dustcart, how was he going to get the flowers back? Ed had told him all the dustcarts took their loads to an enormous dump.

Dirty Bertie

Perhaps Ed would let him hunt through the mountains of rubbish there? Bertie loved the idea of that. But at the end of the road there was no sign of either Ed or the truck. By now it might be miles away. He sped on towards the park and slammed on his brakes at the corner. There, parked a hundred metres away, was the dustcart.

"Hey!" called Bertie. "Hey, wait a minute!"

The truck was starting to pull away. It got up speed, turned a corner and vanished out of sight. Bertie looked down at Whiffer whose ears drooped in sympathy.

He was sunk. Mum would scream. Dad would shout. He would be sent to his room for a million years.

Dirty Bertie

"Bertie, is that you?" called Mum as he crept in through the front door.

"No," answered Bertie.

"I want a word with you. Now."

Bertie drooped into the kitchen where Mum, Dad and Suzy were waiting for him. He could tell by their faces that he'd been rumbled.

Dirty Bertie

"Where are my slippers?" said Dad.

"Where's my Pony Weekly?" asked Suzy.

"And what have you done with my flower arrangement?" demanded Mum.

"Me? Why do I always get the blame?" protested Bertie. "It's not my fault if people keep losing things!"

Mum folded her arms. "Look at me, Bertie. I want the truth. Did you touch those flowers?"

Bertie tried to look at his mum. "I might have um … given them to someone," he mumbled.

"I told you!" said Suzy.

"Who?" demanded Mum.

Bertie tried to think of an answer. He wanted to tell the truth but the truth was he'd given the flowers to a dustcart.

Dirty Bertie

By now they were probably buried
under six feet of cabbages and nappies.

"I gave them to … Gran!" he said with
sudden inspiration.

"Gran? What on earth for?"

"She likes flowers," said Bertie. "She
likes smelling them and stuff."

Mum looked unconvinced. "And when
did you do this?"

"This morning," said Bertie. "I saw
them by the front door and I thought I'd

take them to Gran to cheer her up."

His family stared at him. Bertie had never given flowers to anyone before. On the other hand, he had been known to do all sorts of weird things. Mum's expression softened a bit.

"Well it was a nice thought, Bertie, but I need those flowers back. They've got to be at the church hall by ten. I'll give Gran a ring."

She picked up the phone.

"No!" said Bertie, desperately. "I'll go round! It'll be quicker. She's probably finished smelling them by now."

Mum replaced the phone. "All right, but you'd better hurry. If I miss this competition you're in serious trouble."

Dirty Bertie

Bertie set off with Whiffer padding beside him. At the end of the road he sat down on a wall to think. Now what was he going to do? Bringing Gran into it had only made things worse. Now Mum expected him to come back with her stupid flower arrangement. He stared gloomily at Whiffer who was sniffing around the garden behind him. The house was empty and the front garden overgrown with tall weeds.

Suddenly Bertie had a brilliant idea. What was to stop him making his own

Dirty Bertie

flower arrangement? It would be easy! There were hundreds of flowers right here that nobody wanted. All he had to do was pick a handful, stick them in a pot and enter it in the competition. If he took it to the church hall himself, his mum might never find out.

Half an hour later Bertie had put his plan into operation. The new flower arrangement had been safely delivered to the hall. He hurried home to tell his mum the good news.

CHAPTER 4

The summer fair was in full swing when
Bertie and his family arrived. He trailed
round the stalls with Whiffer on his lead.
There were stalls selling plants and
home-made jam but nothing to interest
Bertie. For some reason, Whiffer kept
whining and pulling him back to the table
displaying the flower arrangements.

Dirty Bertie

Mrs Nicely was standing by the table, talking to Bertie's mum. "I don't know what I'd do if I won again," she was saying. "It would be too embarrassing."

"I can imagine," said Bertie's mum. "So which one is yours?"

"Oh, that little vase of tiger lilies," said Mrs Nicely, pointing to a towering display of yellow blooms. She lowered her voice and pointed. "Can you believe someone actually entered that ghastly mess?"

Dirty Bertie

Bertie stared at the "ghastly mess".
It was a cracked pot with dandelions,
grass and twigs sticking out in all
directions. In the middle was what
looked like a dog's bone.

"Actually," said Bertie, loudly, "I think
that's the best of them all."

Mum pulled him to one side. "Bertie,
where's my flower arrangement?
I thought you said you gave it in."

"Um … I did," said Bertie. Luckily, at that moment, he was interrupted by one of the judges.

"Can I have your attention? We're about to announce the results of the flower arranging competition," he boomed.

Second prize went to Mrs Nicely who tried hard not to look disappointed. First prize went to Mr Pye's bowl of roses.

"Finally," said the judge, "the prize for the most original display. This year we felt one entry beautifully captured our theme of 'Wild Nature'."

The judge held up a pot. It was Bertie's pot. "The winner," he said, "is Mrs Burns."

"That's us!" shouted Bertie, excitedly. Whiffer barked and strained on his lead, trying to reach his bone.

Mum looked at Bertie and then in

horror at the scruffy pot of weeds the
judge was holding. "Bertie, that is *not* my
flower arrangement," she hissed.

"No," admitted Bertie. "I had to make
a few um ... changes."

"Go on," Dad whispered to Mum.
"They're all waiting."

Mum stepped forward to collect her
prize, her face a deep shade of pink.

"Tell me," said the judge. "I'm curious.
What gave you the idea of using a bone?
Most original."

Mum shot a dark look at Bertie. "Oh
it was my son's idea really. He can make
a dog's dinner of anything."

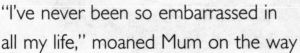

"I've never been so embarrassed in
all my life," moaned Mum on the way

home. "Mrs Nicely looked as if she was going to explode."

Bertie couldn't see what she was complaining about. After all, she wanted to win a prize and she had. You would have thought she'd be grateful! In any case things had worked out pretty well. His mum had won a gardening kit, which included a large pair of green gardening gloves. Bertie was wearing them now. They were the perfect thing for a bin man.

Dirty Bertie

FETCH!

For Julia, Edward and Mickey-Love ~ D R
For Zoe, Ed, Arthur, Maisie and Tess the dog
~ A M

Contents

1   Fetch!   102

2   Royal!   132

3   Wedding!   164

CHAPTER 1

DING DONG.

"Bertie, can you get that?" called Mum.

Bertie scooted into the hall and opened the front door.

"Special delivery!" said the postman, handing him a brown parcel.

It was addressed to Master Bertie Burns. Wait a minute — that was him!

"I GOT A
PRESENT!
I GOT A
PRESENT!" he yelled,
bursting into the kitchen.

"It's not fair!" grumbled Suzy.
"Why didn't *I* get anything?"

"Cos no one likes you," said Bertie,
sticking out his tongue.

Mum was looking at the postmark.
"It must be a late birthday present.
I think it's from Uncle Ed in America."

Bertie gasped. Rich Uncle Ed? He sent
the coolest presents – even if they never
arrived on time.
Bertie tore off the
wrapping paper.
He stared. It *wasn't*!
It *couldn't* be!

Dirty Bertie

"Ha ha! It's a toy dog," said Suzy.

"No it isn't, it's a ROBODOG!" whooped Bertie.

He read the label tied round the collar.

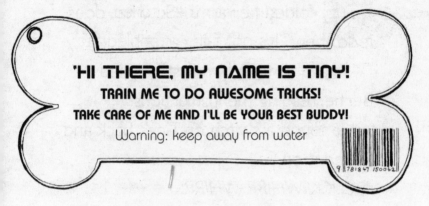

'HI THERE, MY NAME IS TINY!
TRAIN ME TO DO AWESOME TRICKS!
TAKE CARE OF ME AND I'LL BE YOUR BEST BUDDY!
Warning: keep away from water

This was the best present ever! Better even than the prehistoric dino-poop Darren had given him for his birthday. Think of all the things he could do with a robot! Tiny could keep intruders out of Bertie's bedroom. He'd train him to bark at Miss Boot and to bite Know-All Nick. Wait till his friends heard about this –

he'd be the envy of the whole school!

Whiffer trotted over and sniffed Tiny suspiciously. What kind of dog was this? It didn't even *smell* like a dog!

Suzy folded her arms. "So what does it do then?"

"I have to train him first," replied Bertie, reading the instructions.

He found a switch on Tiny's back and flicked it on.

CLICK! WHIRR, WHIRR!

Tiny stirred into life. His eyes flashed red and his head wagged from side to side. Bertie set him on the ground and grabbed the remote control. He pressed a button.

"Sit, Tiny!" he commanded.

BEEP, BEEP! CLICK, CLICK!

Tiny folded his back legs and sat down.

Dirty Bertie

"Amazing!" gasped Dad.

"Wonderful!" said Mum.

Whiffer looked puzzled. No one ever got this excited when *he* sat down.

"Lie down, Tiny!" said Bertie.

WHIRR, CLICK! Tiny lay down.

Now for the big one, thought Bertie.

"Come, Tiny!" he said, patting his knees. "Come to me!"

CLICK, WHIRR! BEEP, BEEP!

Tiny's little legs began to move and he plodded jerkily across the floor.

"Look! He's doing it – he's walking!" cried Bertie.

"Oh, isn't that sweet?" said Mum.

Whiffer growled. He'd seen quite enough. It was time to put this imposter in his place.

GRRR!

He pounced, pinning Tiny to the floor.

Dirty Bertie

BEEP! WHIRR!

GRRR!

"NO, WHIFFER! BAD BOY!" yelled
Bertie, grabbing him by the collar and
yanking him off.

Whiffer hung his head. What had he
done now?

Bertie opened the back door and
shoved him towards it. "OUT!"

WHAM! The door slammed shut.

Whiffer padded to the window and
watched everyone crowd round the
new dog, smiling and clapping. His ears
drooped. What was going on? One
moment he was Bertie's best friend, the
next he'd been replaced by a flat-faced
mutt who walked like a puppet. Well, he
wasn't taking this lying down. He'd show
that pesky pooch who was top dog!

CHAPTER 2

Next morning, Whiffer lay in wait for the postman. Before long a pile of letters thudded on to the mat.

WOOF! WOOF! He bounded into the hall excitedly.

WHIRR, WHIRR! BEEP, BEEP!

Too late – Tiny had got there first. He scooped up the letters in his mouth and trundled past with red eyes flashing. Whiffer drooped after him into the kitchen.

Tiny stopped beside Dad and wagged his tail.

BEEP! RUFF! RUFF!

Dad looked down. "Well, look at this! Tiny's brought the post! Who's a clever boy?"

He patted the little robot on the head and took the letters.

"I've been training him," said Bertie, proudly. "Roll over, Tiny."

Tiny rolled over.

"I must say he's very well behaved." Mum smiled. "Not like *some* dogs I could mention."

"He does everything I tell him," said Bertie. "Watch this!"

He pressed a green button on the remote control. "Dance, Tiny!"

WHIRR, CLICK! ZOOB, ZIB!

Tinny music blared out and Tiny rocked from side to side performing a cute little dance.

"Oh, that's soooo sweet!" cooed Suzy.

Dad looked up from his letter. "Yes and what's more, he doesn't leave hairs on the sofa."

"Or go crazy when the doorbell goes," said Mum.

"And he won't poo on Mrs Nicely's lawn," said Suzy.

They all turned to look at Whiffer.

WOOF! barked Whiffer. *Finally* someone was paying him some attention! His bowl was empty and he was starving. He picked it up and dropped it at Dad's feet. Dad went on reading his letter. Whiffer padded over to Mum. But she was busy talking to Suzy.

What was the matter with everyone? He carried his bowl over to Bertie and plonked it down.

WOOF! he barked, gazing up at Bertie with big, sad eyes. That usually did the trick.

"Not now, Whiffer, I'm busy!" sighed Bertie, fiddling with the remote.

Whiffer stared. What was going on? His bowl was empty! Wasn't anyone going to notice?

After lunch, Darren and Eugene came round to play. Bertie had told them all about Tiny. He took them out into the garden to show off some of Tiny's tricks. Whiffer trailed after them, hoping to play "Fetch" or "Chew the Slipper". Usually Darren made a fuss of him, but today he didn't seem to notice he was there.

"A real robot!" gasped Darren. "You lucky thing!"

"You could teach him to bring you breakfast in bed," said Eugene.

"And do your homework."

Mmm, it was a tempting idea, thought Bertie. But the instruction booklet only listed Ten Top Tricks like "Sit", "Fetch" and "Beg". All the same, that was ten more tricks than Whiffer could do. Whiffer was about as obedient as a lemon meringue. The thing about Tiny was you could take him anywhere. He didn't bark, he didn't whine and he didn't run off chasing squirrels. And best of all, Bertie was the only one of his friends who had a Robodog.

"Show us a trick," said Darren.

"Okay," said Bertie. "Tiny, lie down!"

WHIRR! CLICK! CLICK!

Tiny lay down.

"Good boy!" said Bertie. "Tiny, roll over!"

Tiny rolled over.

"Show me how you beg!"

Tiny sat up and raised both paws. His ears flopped pathetically.

"Wicked!" laughed Darren.

"Brilliant!" cried Eugene.

Whiffer watched in disbelief. This was too much!

WOOF! WOOF! He bounded over and began chasing his tail in circles.

"What's up with him?" asked Darren.

Dirty Bertie

Bertie shrugged. "Dunno. He's been acting weird ever since I got Tiny."

Tiny showed them how he could play dead. He did his little dance. He plodded over to a tree and cocked his leg. Darren and Eugene laughed as if it was the funniest thing they'd ever seen. Whiffer stared. This was so unfair! When *he* weed against the gate he got in big trouble!

"And wait till you see this," said Bertie, picking up a stick.

"Fetch, Tiny!" He threw the stick over Tiny's head. Whiffer saw his chance. He might not be able to dance, but no one was faster at fetching sticks. He leaped past Bertie, bounding after the stick.

WOOF! WOOF!

WOO—

Hey! Someone had him by the collar!

"NO, WHIFFER. Leave it!" shouted Bertie.

WHIRR! BEEP! CLICK, CLICK!

Tiny trundled over and picked up the stick in his mouth. He brought it back to Bertie and dropped it at his feet. Bertie patted his head.

"Clever boy! Who's a good boy?"

Whiffer growled. *GRRR!* Call that a stick? He'd show that stuck-up pup how to fetch. He looked around. Ah ha! What about that giant stick propping up the washing line?

He bounded across the lawn and seized the clothes prop in his mouth.

TWANG! The washing line sagged to the ground, dragging Mum's sheets in the mud.

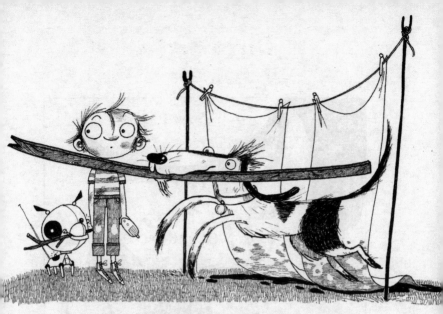

Just at that moment, Mum stuck her head out of the back door.

"Bertie, have you seen my … ARGHH! Look at my washing! It's filthy!"

"It wasn't me!" said Bertie. "It was Whiffer!"

Whiffer tottered over, carrying the giant pole in his mouth. He dropped it at Mum's feet and wagged his tail, looking pleased with himself.

Mum glared at him. "Bad Boy! Get inside!"

CHAPTER 3

Over the next week, Whiffer's behaviour
only got worse. On Tuesday he left a
puddle on the landing. On Wednesday
he hid a filthy bone in Mum and Dad's
bed. On Thursday he tried to bury Tiny's
remote control in the garden. By Friday
Mum and Dad had had enough. They sat
Bertie down for a serious talk.

Dirty Bertie

"This has got to stop," said Mum.

"It can't go on," sighed Dad.

Bertie looked blank. What were they talking about? He hadn't kept worms in his room for ages – at least not anywhere they'd be found.

"What have I done now?" he asked.

"It's not you, it's Whiffer!" said Dad. "He's driving us crazy!"

"He keeps bringing sticks and bones into the house!" said Mum.

"He weed on the carpet!"

"He follows us everywhere!"

"It's not my fault!" grumbled Bertie.

"He's *your* dog," said Dad. "You're supposed to look after him."

"I do!"

"You don't!" said Mum. "Not since you got Tiny. Who took Whiffer to the park this week? Who fed him? Who cleared up his mess?"

Bertie stared at his feet. Perhaps he had neglected Whiffer a bit, but that was because he had so much to do. Tiny was just a puppy and he still needed training. Besides, it was so much fun.

Mum folded her arms. "I'm sorry, Bertie, but this isn't working. Whiffer's *jealous.*"

"JEALOUS?" said Bertie.

"Yes! He doesn't like having another dog around. And you ignoring him only makes it worse!"

"I WON'T ignore him," said Bertie. "I'll look after them both!"

Mum looked at Dad. "All right," she sighed. "We'll give it one more week."

"But Whiffer's got to stop driving us mad," said Dad.

CHAPTER 4

"Whiffer, walkies!"

WOOF! WOOF!

Whiffer flew out of the kitchen and pinned Bertie to the wall. It was ages since they'd gone for walkies. Walkies meant the park and the park meant squirrels.

"Good boy," said Bertie, clipping on his lead. "Tiny's coming too."

Dirty Bertie

Whiffer growled and showed his teeth.
GRRR! Not that mangy little mongrel!

Bertie opened the front door and
Whiffer took off, dragging him down the
path. Tiny wobbled along behind, beeping
and whirring. *This is great*, thought Bertie.
Me and my dogs, all friends together.

The park was full of people walking their dogs. There were tall boxers, yappy terriers and fluffy poodles. But nobody else had a dog like Tiny. The other children crowded around Bertie enviously.

"Wow! Is he yours?" asked a little curly-haired girl.

"Yes," said Bertie. "He's called Tiny.

Want to see him dance?"

Bertie made Tiny perform every one of his tricks. The crowd gasped and clapped. Whiffer looked away, bored.

"Can he fetch my ball?" asked the little girl.

"He can fetch anything," said Bertie, taking the rubber ball. He sent the ball bouncing across the grass.

"Fetch, Tiny!"

Dirty Bertie

CLICK, CLICK! WHIRR! Tiny set off.
But Whiffer had seen the ball too.
In a blur of speed, he overtook the
robot. Seconds later, he was back,
dropping the ball at Bertie's feet and
wagging his tail.

"No!" said Bertie. "Whiffer, stay. Let
Tiny get this one."

Bertie threw the ball as far as he
could. Whiffer forgot all about "Stay" –
he was much better at "Fetch". He set
off, racing past Tiny to get there first.
The ball bounced towards the pond.

DOINK! DOINK! … PLOP!

"TINY, NO, COME BACK…!" yelled
Bertie.

Too late. Whiffer plunged into the
water, scattering ducks in all directions.
Tiny followed, beetling along behind.

Dirty Bertie

Dirty Bertie

SPLASH!

WHIRR, WHIRR! … BEEP! … BLUB BLUB … BLOOP!

Bubbles rose to the surface.

"TINY!" called Bertie. "TINY?"

Silence.

"He can't swim," said the little girl.

Bertie stared.

A moment later Whiffer arrived like a hurricane on four legs and flattened him on the grass. He was muddy, dripping wet and clutching a rubber ball. He dropped it on the grass and barked excitedly.

WOOF! WOOF!

"No! Ha ha! Get off!" giggled Bertie, as Whiffer licked his face.

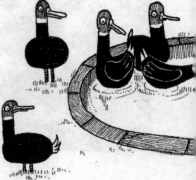

Dirty Bertie

He got up and ruffled Whiffer's fur.
"Good boy," he said. "Tell you what, let's
see if there's any squirrels."

WOOF! Whiffer took off like a furry
bolt of lightning. Bertie ran to catch up.
Tiny had been okay – for a robot – but
there really wasn't anyone like good
old Whiffer!

CHAPTER 1

Bertie opened the front door.

Gran zoomed past him and burst into the kitchen where Mum, Dad and Suzy were having tea. Bertie had never seen her so excited. She looked like she might take off.

"You'll never guess what!" she panted. "I'm going to meet the Queen!"

"No!" gasped Mum.

"Yes!"

"Never!"

"I am. Look – here's the invitation!"

She fished in her handbag and pulled out a silver-trimmed card with an important-looking coat of arms.

Bertie, Suzy, Mum and Dad crowded round to look.

Her Majesty The Queen Graciously Invites

Mrs D. Burns and guest

To a *Royal Garden Party* at BUCKINGHAM PALACE

Saturday 3rd June

(Please Dress Posh)

Dirty Bertie

"Goodness! A royal garden party?" said Mum.

"Isn't it exciting?" said Gran. "I can hardly wait!"

Suzy read the invitation again.

"And guest," she said. "What does that mean?"

"It means I can bring a friend or relative," explained Gran.

"What? To meet the Queen?" asked Bertie, wide-eyed.

"Yes!"

"Actually really MEET her?"

"Yes, actually really."

Bertie could hardly believe his ears. Imagine that – going to a party at the Queen's house! Bertie loved parties and this would be the greatest ever. Think of the food – royal jelly and king-sized ice creams. Think of the games – Musical Thrones, Pass the Diamonds and Hide and Seek with a hundred rooms to choose from. Maybe the Queen would decide to knight him? Maybe she'd even  let him borrow her crown for a day to wear to school? Hang on though, didn't Gran say she could only take *one* guest to the party? And she hadn't said who it would be!

"Let me take your coat, Dotty," said Mum, steering Gran into a chair.

"Are you comfy? I'll get you a cushion!" simpered Suzy.

"Have some cake!" offered Dad, cutting a huge slice of sponge.

Bertie scowled. He could see what his
sneaky family were up to. They wanted
Gran to choose them!

"Well? Have you decided?" asked
Mum.

"Decided what?"

"Who you're taking to the garden
party?"

"Oh yes," said Gran. She dabbed her lips with a napkin. "Well, it wasn't easy, I've got so many friends. But in the end I thought – who do I know that's never been to London? Who's never even seen Buckingham Palace?"

"ME!" yelled Bertie, banging into the table and spilling the cups.

"BERTIE?" gasped Suzy.

"Is that a good idea?" said Dad. "I mean Bertie – meeting the Queen?"

"Why shouldn't I meet her?" demanded Bertie.

"Well, it's just ... sometimes you forget your manners."

"I don't!" said Bertie, grabbing another slice of cake.

Of course there was the time the lady Mayoress visited his school. That was a

Dirty Bertie

bit of a disaster. But it wasn't easy to
shake hands with a bogey stuck to your
finger. Still, Bertie was sure he wouldn't
make the same mistake with the Queen.
She probably had servants to deal with
that sort of thing.

CHAPTER 2

Bertie couldn't wait to tell his friends at school. They were going to be so jealous! He waited until break time when they were out in the playground.

"What are you doing next Saturday?" he said.

Darren shrugged. "Nothing."

"I've got swimming," said Donna.

Dirty Bertie

"I've got to visit my aunt," said Eugene, gloomily.

"Oh. Only I won't be here," said Bertie. "I've got to go to London. To meet the Queen."

The others stared at him boggle-eyed. Darren burst out laughing.

"YOU? MEET THE QUEEN? HA HA!"

"Good one, Bertie," grinned Eugene. "For a minute I almost believed you."

"It's *true*!" said Bertie. "She's giving a gardening party. Me and Gran are invited."

"Invited to what?" asked a drawling voice. Bertie groaned. Trust Know-All Nick to poke his nose in where it wasn't wanted!

"Bertie reckons he's going to meet the Queen," grinned Darren.

Dirty Bertie

"Oh ha ha, very funny," sneered Nick.

"I am!" said Bertie.

"Liar liar, pants on fire!"

"All right, don't believe me," said Bertie, huffily.

"I don't," said Nick.

"Okay, I'll bring you the invitation."

"Huh! Anyone could write an invitation," scoffed Nick. "Prove you met the Queen, then I might believe you."

"Right, I will!" said Bertie. "I'll get her photo. We'll soon see who's lying!"

The week went by slowly. As the big day drew near, Bertie's parents gave him lots of helpful advice.

"Don't mumble!" said Dad.

"Don't slouch!" said Mum.

"And please, please, please DON'T PICK YOUR NOSE!"

"I'm not going to," sighed Bertie. Anyone would think he had no manners at all!

Mum pulled up a chair. "All right, let's have a practice. Pretend I'm the Queen

Dirty Bertie

and we've just met. Now, what do
you say?"

"Um... Where's the food?" said Bertie.

"You can't ask the Queen that!"

"Why not? I'll be hungry."

"You have to make Polite
Conversation," said Mum. "And
remember to call her 'Your Majesty'.
Now try again. Ahem...
Good afternoon, young
man."

"Good hafternoon, Your
Magicsty," said Bertie.
Mum gave him a look.

Dirty Bertie

"Why are you talking like that?"

"I'm makin' polite what-you-said."

"You sound like you've got a mouthful of chewing gum. Speak normally! And stop bobbing up and down!"

"I'm bowing!" said Bertie.

"Well don't! Keep still and talk to me. And hurry up, the Queen hasn't got all day!"

"Good afternoon, Your Magicsty," said Bertie. "Um, when do we eat?"

Mum gave up. There would be hundreds of people at the garden party. With any luck, Bertie wouldn't get within a mile of the Queen. She certainly hoped not.

CHAPTER 3

The great day finally dawned. At ten o'clock on Saturday morning, Bertie knocked on Gran's front door. Gran did a double take. Was this really her grandson? Bertie's face shone, his hair was neatly parted and he was wearing a tie.

"My goodness!" she cried. "I hardly

recognized you. You look as if you've been polished!"

Gran took his picture. Then Bertie took a picture of Gran in her new dress and hat. Then they set off for the station.

Just after two o'clock they presented themselves at the palace gates. A man wearing a smart uniform showed them through to the biggest garden Bertie had ever seen. It had wide green lawns, magnificent fountains and statues with bare bottoms. Across the lawn, hundreds of people were spilling out of an enormous white tent.

Bertie stared. How was he going to meet the Queen with all this lot?

Inside the tent, things didn't get any better. He could hardly move without treading on someone's foot or being poked by a handbag. Bertie sighed. Where was the party food? The royal jelly and ice cream? A waiter passed by with a tray of dainty cucumber sandwiches. Bertie took one and crammed it into his mouth. It would hardly have fed a goldfish.

He looked around. This was going to be the worst party ever. Everyone was nearly as old as Gran – and all they did was stand around talking and sipping tea. Worst of all, the Queen hadn't even bothered to turn up! Bertie had been keeping an eye out for someone wearing a sparkly gold crown, but there was no sign of her. At this rate he would never get a photo. What would he tell all his friends?

Dirty Bertie

"BERTIE!" hissed Gran.

"What?"

"Don't eat so fast. And don't say 'what?' say 'pardon'."

"But I didn't burp!" protested Bertie. He sighed. "Can I see if there's any cake?"

Gran rolled her eyes. "If you must. But don't be greedy."

Bertie pushed his way through the crowd until he spotted a waiter with a plate of cakes. There were dainty cupcakes, macaroons and lemon slices. He tugged on the waiter's sleeve, and started to fill his plate. A voice interrupted him.

"Are you having a nice time?"

Bertie turned to see a lady in a pale blue dress, with a matching hat. She was about Gran's age, but spoke terribly nicely, as if she was reading the news.

"Er, yes ... yes thanks," said Bertie.

"One imagines this might not be your cup of tea," said the smiling lady.

"Oh, I don't drink tea," said Bertie. "I tried it once but I spat it out."

"I meant the garden party. Are you really having a nice time?"

"Honestly?" said Bertie, cramming a cupcake into his mouth.

"Honestly."

Bertie lowered his voice. "It's dead boring. There's nothing to do."

"Ah," said the lady. "I see."

"I mean look!" said Bertie, spraying cake crumbs everywhere. "You'd think the Queen'd do better than this. There aren't even any balloons or games! She could at least have got a bouncy castle!"

The lady seemed to find this idea amusing. "People would have to take off their hats," she said.

Bertie caught sight of Gran, who seemed to be trying to tell him something. She pointed at Bertie's companion and waved her hands as if she was swatting flies. Bertie hadn't a clue what she meant. He'd only taken four cakes so he was hardly being greedy.

Other people were waiting to meet the lady in the blue hat. She seemed surprisingly popular.

"Well, I enjoyed our little chat," she said. "Tell me, are you fond of dogs?"

"Um, yes, I've got a dog," said Bertie. "He's called Whiffer."

"I have corgis. Five. Molly, Polly, Vicky, Georgia and Jemima. Perhaps you'd like to see them?"

"Me?" said Bertie.

"Yes, my footman will show you the way."

A man in a black uniform bowed. Bertie wondered why the lady had a footman. Maybe she had bad feet? In any case, dogs were much more interesting than people. He followed the footman out of the tent to a small courtyard. A maid stood waiting with five fat little corgis, all pulling on their leads.

CHAPTER 4

Bertie let the corgis lick the cake crumbs off his hand.

"You like dogs?" asked the maid.

"Yes," replied Bertie. "Do you?"

"Can't stand 'em. Smelly, yappy things. Want to hold them for a bit?"

"Can I?"

Bertie took the leads from the maid,

who seemed glad of a break. Molly, Polly, Vicky, Georgia and Jemima sniffed round his legs.

"They haven't had their walkies yet," said the maid.

"I could take them," said Bertie. "I'm not doing anything."

The maid considered. "Okay, just round the gardens. But keep 'em on the lead."

Bertie set off. He was used to taking Whiffer for walks, but five excited corgis were a lot more trouble. They pulled in different directions and their leads got tangled under his feet. They crossed the lawn, passing the Queen's garden party. Ooops! Bertie stumbled over a tap.

WHOOSH! A garden sprinkler came on, spraying him with jets of water.

"Arghh! Oooh!" yelped Bertie, letting go of the dog leads.

Free at last, the corgis bolted through a flower bed and raced across the lawn.

"NO! COME BACK!" yelled Bertie, as they headed for the door of the big white tent.

Dirty Bertie

He chased after them. The party was still in full flow, but as he reached the tent he heard a terrible noise.

WOOF! CRASH! TINKLE! THUNK!

Bertie barged his way through the crowd. He stared in horror. A waiter was lying on the floor, surrounded by broken cups and plates. Five fat little corgis were clambering over him, licking up cream and bits of cupcake.

"Crumbs!" gasped Bertie.

Dirty Bertie

The party had fallen silent. The waiter scrambled to his feet and bowed to the lady in the blue hat.

"Your Majesty, I'm most terribly sorry," he said.

Dirty Bertie

Bertie gaped. "Your *Majesty?*" Then the lady in the blue hat was the QUEEN? Why hadn't anyone warned him? He'd told her that her party was boring. He'd let her dogs loose and broken her best plates. She would probably have his head chopped off!

The Queen turned to Bertie and raised her eyebrows.

"Ah," she said. "And what do you have to say for yourself?"

Bertie gulped. He bowed low.

"Your Magicsty … um, would you be in a photo?"

Dirty Bertie

The following Monday, Bertie's friends were waiting for him in the playground. They hadn't forgotten his ridiculous boast.

"So?" grinned Darren. "How was the party?"

"Did you see the palace?" asked Eugene.

"And did you meet her Majesty?" jeered Know-All Nick.

Bertie waited for them to stop laughing. "Actually, I did," he said. "We had a good chat."

"Liar!" snorted Nick. "You're making it up."

"Am I," said Bertie. He reached into his pocket and brought out a photo.

Nick stared. His mouth fell open. He turned white, then green.

"You can keep it if you like," said Bertie. "I've got lots!"

WEDDING!

CHAPTER 1

Bertie groaned.

"It's not fair! Why do I have to go?"

"It's your cousin's wedding," said Mum.

"I love weddings," sighed Suzy. "So romantic!"

"Yuck! I hate them!" said Bertie.

The last wedding his parents had dragged him to was deathly dull. He had to sit through speeches that went on for days. Even when it was time to leave there were armies of aunts waiting to kiss him. This time, his cousin Dora was marrying her fiancé, Bruce. Bertie had met drippy Dora. He couldn't see why anyone would want to talk to her – let alone marry her.

"In any case, we're going," said Mum. "Suzy's a bridesmaid and you're a pageboy."

Bertie looked horrified. *Him*? A pageboy?

"No way!" he cried.

"All you have to do is look smart," said Mum.

"I *never* look smart," said Bertie, truthfully.

"You will for Dora's wedding," said

Dirty Bertie

Mum firmly. "That's why I'm taking you shopping on Saturday. Suzy can find a bridesmaid's dress and we'll get you a kilt."

"A KILT?" Bertie gasped for air. "But that's a … a…"

"A SKIRT!" giggled Suzy. "HA HA!"

"Don't be silly," said Mum. "Bruce is Scottish and lots of the men will be wearing kilts."

"But can't I just wear jeans?" begged Bertie.

"Of course not! It's a wedding!"

Bertie groaned. This was torture! Cruelty! It couldn't be happening!

Dirty Bertie

On Saturday morning Mum took them
to "Gladrags" wedding shop in town. The
snooty assistant helped them to choose
things to try on. Suzy picked a pretty lilac
dress with puff sleeves and went to
change. Bertie didn't choose anything.
The kilts were all too big, too baggy, too
… skirty! In the end Mum chose one for
him. Bertie took it into the changing
room and slammed the door.

A moment later, Suzy appeared.

"Oh darling, you look lovely!" said
Mum.

Suzy twirled round in front of the
mirror. She'd always dreamed of being a
bridesmaid. It was just a pity Bertie
would be there to spoil the pictures.

"Where is Bertie?" Mum frowned.
"He's been in there ages."

She knocked on the changing room
door. "BERTIE?"

"He's not here!"

"Bertie, hurry up, we're waiting!"

Dirty Bertie

"It doesn't fit. It's too big!" grumbled Bertie.

"Nonsense! Let me see!" said Mum.

"NO!"

Mum folded her arms. "Right, I'm counting to three. One, two, thr—"

BLAM! The door burst open. Bertie stomped out, scowling furiously. He was wearing a black jacket, a frilly shirt and a green kilt with a hairy sporran. It was the smallest kilt in the shop, but it practically reached Bertie's ankles.

"It's too big!" he moaned. "I look stupid!"

"Ahh," said Suzy. "Do you want an ickle pink bow for your hair?"

"SHUT UP!" cried Bertie.

"Take no notice," said Mum. "Lots of boys wear kilts. I think you look very handsome."

Bertie scowled at his reflection in the mirror. Handsome? He couldn't go out like this! What if one of his friends saw him? It was bad enough that he had to be at Dora's wedding, but dressed in a tartan skirt? No, he wouldn't do it, not for his cousin, not for anyone. And there was nothing they could do to make him.

CHAPTER 2

Bertie climbed into the car and slumped on the back seat. It was the morning of Bruce and Dora's wedding. He had tried everything to get out of wearing the horrible hairy kilt. First he'd claimed it was torn, then lost, then that it'd fallen down the toilet. Mum wasn't fooled. She said he was wearing the kilt and he'd better get used to it.

The cars set off for the church. Bertie was going with Suzy and Neil, the best man. Bertie wriggled around. His kilt was itchy. He tucked it between his legs. He hoped it wasn't a windy day. Dad said that Scots didn't wear anything under their kilts – but he wasn't falling for that one! He was wearing two pairs of pants, just in case.

"Move over!" grumbled Suzy.

"You move over!" said Bertie.

"No! You're creasing my dress!"

Neil groaned. "Stop squabbling! You're giving me a headache!"

Bertie rolled his eyes. What a fusspot! If Bertie ever needed a best man it wouldn't be Neil.

Neil looked at his watch. He checked

he had his hanky and his speech.
He checked he'd got the ring in the
little box.

"What's that?" asked Bertie.

"The wedding ring, stupid," said Suzy.

"Can I see it?"

"Certainly not!" said Neil.

"Please. Please, please, please…"

"Oh all right," groaned Neil. "Just be
careful!"

Bertie opened the box. "Wow!" he
gasped. "Is it real gold?"

"Of course it's real!"

Bertie had never actually held
a real gold ring. The only rings he
ever got were out of Christmas crackers.
Dora must have small hands because this
ring was tiny. Bertie held it up. Maybe it
would fit him? He slipped it over his

thumb to see.

"BERTIE!" snapped Neil. "Give it back."

"Okay, okay," sighed Bertie. Some people were so impatient!

He pulled at the ring. Oops! It wouldn't come off. He tried to twist it. Argh! He tugged. He wrestled and wriggled. It wouldn't budge.

"Bertie, come ON!" groaned Neil.

"I'm … trying!" panted Bertie. "It seems to be … arrrr … stuck!"

Dirty Bertie

The car turned a corner and pulled up outside the church. They all climbed out. In desperation Neil and Suzy took it in turns to try and pull the ring off Bertie's thumb.

"Keep still!"

"I am ... OW! That hurts!" moaned Bertie.

It was no use. The ring was stuck like superglue. No matter how much they pulled and yanked, it wouldn't come off. A car drew up and Mum and Dad got out.

"Everything okay?" said Dad.

"It's Bertie," said Suzy. "He was playing with the ring and now he's got it stuck!"

"What?"

Bertie held up his thumb to show them.

Dirty Bertie

"It's not my fault!" he grumbled. "How was I to know it wouldn't come off?"

"Of course it's your fault," cried Neil. "You should never have touched it in the first place."

He paced up and down in a panic. This was terrible, a nightmare! Everyone was in the church waiting, and any minute now Dora would be here. But how could they start the service without a ring?

Dad checked his watch. "What are we going to do?"

Mum had an idea. "Butter!" she cried.

"What?"

"Butter – that's how you get it off! Rub his thumb with butter."

"We don't have any butter!" groaned Neil.

"What about the church hall?" said Suzy.

"Of course!" said Mum. Everyone was going to the church hall after the service for the wedding party. There would be stacks of food. They were bound to find butter somewhere.

Just then, a big white car drew up outside the church. The bride had arrived. Dora got out, trailing vast clouds of silk. Mum sprang into action.

Dirty Bertie

"Quick," she said. "I'll try to delay them.
Bertie, run to the hall with Dad."

"Me? What for?" said Bertie.

"To find some butter!" cried Mum.

"And for heaven's sake, HURRY!"

CHAPTER 3

Bertie and Dad ran to the church hall.
It was empty. The room was set out with
chairs and tables ready for the wedding
party. At the far end was a long table
with drinks and nibbles for the guests.
Bertie's eyes lit up. He hadn't eaten
anything since breakfast.

"Right," said Dad. "You look in here,

Dirty Bertie

Bertie. I'll try the kitchen."

Dad hurried off. Bertie gazed hungrily at the nibbles. He helped himself to a handful of crisps, just to help him think. What had Mum said? Oh yes, butter. Where did they keep the butter? He searched the table. Peanuts, dips, sausage rolls – but no butter.

"Find any?" shouted Dad, clattering cupboard doors in the kitchen.

"No, not yet!"

Bertie grabbed some more crisps in case the service went on a bit. Luckily his sporran was the perfect place to keep a snack. He checked to see Dad wasn't watching. Wait, what was this? Bruce and Dora's

wedding cake was sitting on a trolley.
Bertie loved cake, and this one was
a monster. It was a three cake tower
trimmed with pink roses. On the bottom
cake, written in icing, it said:

Congrats on Your Wonderful Day

Dirty Bertie

Bertie stared. Icing – of course! Icing was just like butter. His finger hovered over the beautiful wedding cake. Should he? Time was running out and he had to get the ring off. This was his last chance. SHHLUPP! Bertie scooped up a big splodge of icing.

Mmm – not bad! He tried a pink rose. *Mmm mmm mmm.*

Remembering his mum's advice, he slathered his thumb in icing and licked it off. Whoops! The writing on the cake had got a bit smudged. Some of the letters were missing. But what about the ring? He twisted it. YES! It slid over his thumb. Genius!

"Any luck, Bertie?" cried Dad, suddenly appearing from the kitchen.

Bertie stood in front of the cake.

Dirty Bertie

"Oh ... um, yes. Look, I got it off!"

He held up the ring triumphantly.

"Thank goodness!" said Dad. "You found some butter?"

"Er, sort of," said Bertie.

"Then what are we standing here for?" said Dad. "Let's get back to the church!"

Bertie glanced over his shoulder at the cake as he left. It did look a bit messy. But it was too late to do anything about it now. After all, it was only a cake. Who was going to notice?

CHAPTER 4

They reached the church and stood
outside, panting for breath. Dad put his
ear to the door. He groaned.

"They've already started!"

"What?" cried Bertie. "They can't
have!"

"They obviously couldn't wait! We'll
have to sneak in quietly," said Dad.

"But what about the ring?" said Bertie, holding it up.

"Give it to Neil! Just try not to draw attention to yourself."

Inside the church, Dora and Bruce stood at the altar. The vicar was reaching the part with the wedding vows. Neil wiped a drop of sweat from his forehead. Where in the name of heaven was Bertie? If he didn't get here soon it would be too late!

"Dora Lara Spooner," said the vicar, "do you take this man to be your husband?"

"I do," trilled Dora.

"Bruce John McDougal, do you take this woman to be your wife?"

"I do," boomed Bruce.

Dirty Bertie

Dirty Bertie

There was a long pause.

"The ring!" whispered the vicar.

"Oh, um, yes, the ring..." stammered Neil, turning bright pink. He searched his pockets as if that might help.

"Neil!" hissed Dora.

Neil shook his head helplessly. "I ... er ... I haven't..."

Dirty Bertie

CRASH!

Every head in the church turned round to look. Bertie had zoomed up the aisle and skidded, falling flat on his face. His kilt had flopped over, so everyone got a good view of his pants. Suzy giggled.

"BERTIE!" hissed Neil.

Bertie got up. He pulled down his kilt and came forward. In his hand was something pink and sticky like a half-sucked sweet. He handed it over. Bruce slid the ring over Dora's finger.

"EUGH!" said Dora.

After the service they all crowded into the church hall for the wedding party. Bertie had to sit through hours of boring speeches, but he didn't care. He was off the hook. Dora grumbled that he'd almost ruined her big day, but Bruce patted his head and said no harm was done.

Neil stood up and banged on the table with a spoon.

"And now, the bride and groom will cut the cake!"

Dirty Bertie

Bertie gulped. Oh no! The cake – he'd forgotten all about it!

A lady pushed the trolley to the front where the bride and groom stood waiting. Dora took the knife ready to cut the first slice. She stared. She gasped. She looked like she might faint.

Her beautiful wedding cake – ruined! The tower was looking wonky, and there were sticky fingermarks all over it. Someone had scoffed most of the pink roses. Worst of all, the message was missing some letters, so now it read:

Wo rats on Your ful Day

Dirty Bertie

"EEEK! MY CAKE!" shrieked Dora.

Mum and Dad turned round. There was only one person who could have done this, and he was wearing a sticky kilt and a guilty expression.

"BERTIE!" groaned Mum.

Bertie gulped. He put his hand into his sporran.

"Um … anyone want a crisp?"

For Felix and Josh ~ D R
For Niav, who has all the Bertie books
~ A M

Contents

1   Trouble!   196

2   Sleepover!   226

3   Bully!   258

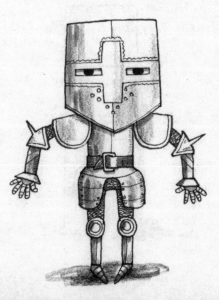

CHAPTER 1

It was another Monday morning. Bertie and his friends were walking to school.

"So what did you do yesterday?" asked Bertie.

"Mostly homework," sighed Eugene. "We've got that maths test, remember?"

Bertie stopped in his tracks.

"Maths test?" he said. "When?"

Dirty Bertie

"Today!" said Eugene. "Miss Boot's testing us on our homework."

"Don't tell me you've forgotten?" said Darren.

Bertie nodded – of course he'd forgotten. He'd meant to do the homework but there'd been so many other things to do, like watch TV.

"Trust you, Bertie!" grinned Darren. "How are you going to pass the test?"

Bertie shrugged. "I'll just have to guess like last time."

He hated maths tests. Why couldn't Miss Boot test him on something he knew – like the world record for burping?

"Maybe she'll have forgotten," he suggested.

"Huh! Not Miss Boot," said Eugene.

Dirty Bertie

"Well, maybe she'll be away then," said Bertie. "Mr Weakly's always off sick."

But when they arrived Miss Boot was there as usual. Bertie couldn't remember her ever missing a day of school. Germs were probably too scared to go near her.

Dirty Bertie

"Well, I hope you all remembered your homework," she said. "I promised you a maths test so we can all look forward to it after break."

Bertie slumped back in his chair. He was doomed. Everyone apart from him seemed to have done their homework. Know-All Nick had probably spent the whole weekend revising. Bertie knew his mum would go mad if she found out he'd watched TV instead of doing his schoolwork. There had to be some way he could get out of the test!

Just then he caught sight of Miss Boot's coffee flask poking out of her bag. It gave him a brilliant idea. What if he could make a magic potion? It always worked in stories, especially if you went to Hogwarts. Magic potions could do all sorts of things, such as making a test disappear! And luckily he was brilliant at magic. His gran had given him a magic set and he'd already learned to make a plastic ball vanish from a cup. All he had to do was make the maths test vanish from Miss Boot's mind! How hard could it be?

Dirty Bertie

The tricky part was getting Miss Boot to drink the magic potion, but that was where the flask came in. If he could somehow sneak the potion into her flask, she'd drink it just like coffee. Bertie sat back – the plan *had* to work. It was his only chance.

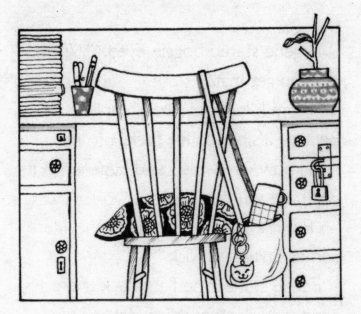

CHAPTER 2

The bell went for break and everyone
filed out. This was Bertie's chance. Miss
Boot was busy preparing the test papers.
Her bag hung from her chair, unguarded.
As Bertie walked past, he grabbed the
flask and stuffed it under his jumper.

Outside he showed Darren and
Eugene his prize.

Dirty Bertie

Eugene stared boggle-eyed. "Where did you get that?"

"From Miss Boot's bag," replied Bertie. "It's her coffee flask."

"I know what it is!" said Eugene. "But what are *you* doing with it?"

"Put it away!" warned Darren. "Here comes Know-All Nick."

Bertie stuffed the flask back under his jumper. Nick stopped to stare at him suspiciously.

"What have you got there?" he demanded.

"Nothing," said Bertie. "And it's none of your business, anyway."

Dirty Bertie

"Really?" said Nick. "If you say so."

They waited for him to leave, then Bertie explained his master plan.

"A magic potion? You think that'll work?" grinned Darren.

"Why not? I'm great at magic," said Bertie.

"You're mad," said Eugene. "If Miss Boot finds out you've taken her flask she'll go potty."

"She won't. I'll put it back after break," said Bertie. "She won't suspect a thing."

"She will when she drinks her coffee!" laughed Darren.

"But then the potion will work," said Bertie. "And the test will vanish from her head like magic!"

Eugene shook his head. "I still say you're crazy. You risk it if you want, but count me out. My mum says you always get me into trouble."

He walked off.

Bertie stared for a moment then turned to Darren. "What about you?"

"I'm in!" Darren smiled. "I'll do anything to avoid a maths test!"

Bertie wasn't exactly sure what ingredients they needed for a magic potion. Obviously bats' wings or dragons' claws would be ideal but they weren't easy to find in the playground. Instead he collected a handful of nettles and dandelions while Darren found a spider's web. Bertie squished them all into Miss Boot's flask. He added water from the drinking fountain and gave it a good shake. They stared at the gloopy liquid.

"YUCK! It looks disgusting!" said
Darren. "She'll never drink that."

"Maybe not," agreed Bertie. "We
need to make it look more like coffee."

He found a puddle and scooped up
a handful of mud. In it went turning the
potion a murky brown.

"That's better. Now what?" asked
Darren.

"Now we make a spell to add the

magic," replied Bertie.

He thought for a moment before shutting his eyes. He circled his hands over the potion, chanting in a low voice:

"Hocus-pocus, pants and vest,
Make Miss Boot forget this test."

Dirty Bertie

"That should do it," said Bertie.

"Great, but what if she doesn't drink it?" frowned Darren.

"She will," said Bertie. "She always has a coffee in the morning."

"First we'll have to get her flask back," Darren pointed out.

"True," said Bertie. "You keep her talking while I sneak it into her bag."

When the bell went, they filed into school and waited for Miss Boot outside the classroom. Soon she came marching down the corridor. Bertie stared. Oh no, she was carrying her bag – she must have taken it with her to the staffroom! How could he put the flask back now? But it was too late to change the plan because Darren had stepped out to stop her.

"Oh, miss, I think Nick's stuck up a tree," he said.

"A tree? What are you talking about?" snapped Miss Boot.

Bertie didn't wait to hear Darren's unlikely explanation. He slipped into the classroom and looked around. Where could he leave the flask so Miss Boot would find it? In a panic he left it on her chair and hurried to his seat.

Seconds later, Miss Boot walked in.

"Hurry up and sit down," she said, thumping her bag down on her desk.

Bertie gave Darren a nod as he took his seat beside him.

Miss Boot glared. "Before we start, has anyone seen my coffee flask?" she demanded. "It was in my bag this morning but now seems to have disappeared."

Dirty Bertie

The class shook their heads. Miss
Boot scowled. Someone had to know
something, she was sure of it. She pulled
out her chair and did a double take. The
flask was right there on her seat. She
certainly hadn't left it there, because she
always took her coffee to the staffroom.
She narrowed her eyes.
*Someone is playing
tricks,* she thought.
*And whoever is responsible,
I will find out.*

CHAPTER 3

Miss Boot was busy explaining the maths test to the class.

"Well?" whispered Eugene. "Did you do it?"

Bertie pointed to the flask.

"Seriously? You've put a magic potion in there?" asked Eugene.

"You missed all the fun," said Bertie.

Dirty Bertie

"And the best part is it looks exactly like coffee!"

"You're bonkers," said Eugene. "What did you put in it?"

Bertie shrugged. "Just the usual potion stuff – nettles, cobwebs, a bit of mud…"

"MUD?" squeaked Eugene. "What if she drinks it?"

"She's meant to drink it," said Bertie. "Otherwise it won't work."

Eugene shook his head. Bertie had done some crazy things in his time but this beat them all.

"She'll probably be sick!" he said.

"She won't," snorted Bertie.

"She will if it's full of mud and cobwebs!" said Eugene. "What if you make her ill?"

Bertie looked a little worried.

Dirty Bertie

"It's only a magic potion," he said.

"Yes, but how do you know what it'll do?" said Eugene. "Her hair might fall out or her tongue could turn blue. Anything could happen! What if she grows horns or something?"

Bertie hadn't thought of this. In stories magic sometimes had unexpected results. He only wanted Miss Boot to forget the maths test, not to sprout horns! Surely a little mud and cobwebs couldn't do any real harm?

Dirty Bertie

On the other hand they'd added weeds, nettles and who knew what. What if the potion did make her ill? He stared at the flask sitting on Miss Boot's desk. He was starting to think this wasn't such a great idea after all.

Just then Miss Boot finished what she was saying and picked up her flask. Bertie watched in horror as she started to unscrew the lid! He had to stop her before it was too late!

CHAPTER 4

Bertie's hand shot up.

"Yes!" groaned Miss Boot. "What is it, Bertie?"

"Can we open a window?" asked Bertie, playing for time.

"A window? What for?" said Miss Boot.

"I'm too hot," moaned Bertie. "I'm

216

burning up!"

Miss Boot rolled her eyes.

"Is anyone else too hot?" she asked.

No one was. Nevertheless she set down her flask and went to open a window. Anything so they could get on with the test in peace.

Back at her desk she picked up the pile of papers.

"Right, let's get started," she said. "Nicholas, hand round these test papers, please."

Bertie breathed out. Miss Boot seemed to have forgotten her coffee – at least for the moment.

He tried to stay calm. Facing the maths test was bad enough, but now he couldn't take his eyes off Miss Boot. Sooner or later she'd remember she

Dirty Bertie

was gasping for coffee and then what would happen? He imagined her drinking the potion and turning as green as a frog.

Know-All Nick set a test paper down on Bertie's desk.

"Feeling nervous, Bertie?" he smirked. "I do hope you've done your homework!"

"Course I have," lied Bertie.

Nick moved on to the next desk.

Dirty Bertie

"What on earth are you going to do?" hissed Eugene.

"About what?" asked Darren.

"The potion!" said Eugene.

"Eugene thinks it'll make Miss Boot sick," said Bertie. "What if her hair falls out?"

"HA HA!" laughed Darren. "It won't, will it?"

"How should I know?" moaned Bertie. "I've never made a magic potion before! It could do anything."

"SILENCE!" boomed Miss Boot. "There should be no need for talking. Right, you may all turn over your papers and begin."

Bertie read the first few questions. He hadn't the faintest idea what they meant. In any case, he had other things to worry about. He watched Miss Boot anxiously. Oh no, she was reaching for her flask again! She unscrewed the lid and placed the cup on her desk.

Bertie's hand shot up once more.

"What is it now?" groaned Miss Boot. "This better be important, Bertie."

"Um … can I get you a glass of water?" asked Bertie. "You must be thirsty doing all that talking."

"I've got my coffee, thank you," snapped Miss Boot.

"But water's better for you," argued Bertie.

"ENOUGH!" thundered Miss Boot. "Stop wasting time and get on with the test!"

Bertie gulped. He'd tried but it was hopeless. He watched in alarm as Miss

Dirty Bertie

Boot poured the murky brown liquid into her cup. Surely she'd notice that something wasn't right? But Miss Boot was too busy keeping an eye on her class. She raised the cup to her lips and took a large gulp. Bertie held his breath…

"BLEURGH!"

Miss Boot spat the drink all over her desk. She stared down at her cup. Gloopy bits of something swam around on top.

"What on earth is this?" she spluttered.

Bertie gulped. At least Miss Boot hadn't turned green or sprouted horns. She rose to her feet. The class had all stopped writing.

"Whatever this is, it is *not* coffee," she said. "Somebody in this class has been playing tricks. At break time my flask went missing. One of you took it – WHO WAS IT?"

There was a terrible silence. Bertie slid down in his seat. *As long as no one talks, she can't prove anything*, he thought.

Dirty Bertie

Know-All Nick raised his hand.

"Please, miss, I think I know," he bleated. "At break I saw Bertie hiding something under his jumper. It looked like your flask."

Bertie closed his eyes. Trust blabbermouth Nick to ruin everything.

"BERTIE!" thundered Miss Boot. "Did you put something in my coffee?"

"Um … not exactly," squeaked Bertie.

"Then what, *exactly*?" demanded Miss Boot.

"I might have swapped your coffee for something else," admitted Bertie. "A sort of … um … magic potion."

Miss Boot's eyebrows shot up.

"A WHAT?"

"A magic potion," repeated Bertie. "It was nothing bad – just weeds, cobwebs and a bit of mud."

"MUD?" screeched Miss Boot. "You put mud in my coffee?"

"Just a little," said Bertie. "I only wanted you to forget the maths test."

"Ah, so now we're getting to the truth," said Miss Boot grimly. "Well, I hate to disappoint you, Bertie, but magic potions won't save you. You're going to take this test – not only today, but every day until you get full marks."

"*Full marks?*" groaned Bertie.

"That's right. And to help, here's a little light reading for homework," said Miss Boot, handing him an enormous book. "I'm sure it'll work like magic."

SLEEPOVER!

CHAPTER 1

Bertie's mum had taken him clothes shopping in town. They were just leaving Dibble's department store when Bertie stopped dead. A pale, smug-faced boy was heading their way with his mother. It was his sworn enemy, Know-All Nick.

Bertie tried to duck behind his mum but it was too late…

Dirty Bertie

"Hello, Bertie!" sang Nick.

"Hello, Nickerless," replied Bertie with a scowl.

"How lovely to bump into you!" trilled Nick's mum. "We haven't seen you since last parents' evening. And how is Bertie getting on at school?"

"Oh … yes, very well, thank you, Mrs Wormsley," said Mum.

This was news to Bertie. His last report was so bad he'd tried to lose it in the postbox.

"Of course, Nicholas is doing wonderfully well," Mrs Wormsley boasted. "We've just popped in to buy him a little treat for passing his piano exam, haven't we, poppet?"

Poppet? Bertie raised his eyebrows. Nick stuck out his tongue. The two

mums carried on chatting and took out
their phones to swap numbers.

"What's in the shopping bag?" asked
Nick.

"None of your business," replied
Bertie.

Nick snatched the bag.

"Ooh, new pants!" he jeered. "Spotty
ones to match your face!"

"Give them back!" cried Bertie. "Anyway, what are you buying? Ugly cream?"

"Actually, I'm getting a new ski jacket," bragged Nick. "We're going skiing after Christmas. I bet you've never been."

"Course I have," snorted Bertie. At least he'd been to the Snowdome, which obviously counted. He tugged at his mum's arm to go.

"Yes, all right, Bertie," said Mum. "We'd better get on. Lovely to see you."

"You too, and I'll be in touch," replied Nick's mum.

"What was all that about?" asked Bertie as they hurried away.

"Oh, she suggested you might like to

go for a sleepover some time," replied Mum.

A SLEEPOVER? Bertie almost walked into a lamppost.

"A sleepover – *with Nick?*" he wailed.

"Yes, it was kind of her, wasn't it?" said Mum.

"But it's Know-All Nick!" said Bertie. "I'm not going for a sleepover at his house!"

"Why not?" asked Mum.

"Because we're not even friends!" cried Bertie. "We're more like deadly enemies. Surely you know that?"

Dirty Bertie

"Well, I know he's not one of your best friends, but you are in the same class," said Mum.

"Loads of people are in my class but it doesn't make them my friends!" protested Bertie. "Nick's a know-all and a big head and he's always telling tales."

"I'm sure he isn't," said Mum. "Anyway, its only a sleepover. I could hardly say you wouldn't go."

"WHY NOT?" demanded Bertie.

Mum sighed. "Don't make such a fuss, Bertie. I expect his mum was just being polite. She'll probably forget she ever mentioned it."

Bertie certainly hoped so. A sleepover … at Know-All Nick's house? He'd rather sleep in a cave with vampire bats!

CHAPTER 2

The following week Bertie was getting ready for school. Downstairs he could hear his mum talking on her phone.

"Yes, thank you, I'm sure Bertie will be delighted."

He hurried down.

"Who was that?"

"That was Mrs Wormsley," said Mum.

Dirty Bertie

"She's invited you for a sleepover with Nick this Friday."

Bertie's mouth fell open.

"You didn't say 'yes', did you?" he gulped.

"What else could I say?" asked Mum.

"Anything! Phone her back," begged Bertie. "Say I'm sick, say I've got toothache or brainache or something."

"I'm not telling lies," said Mum. "It's just for one night, it's not going to kill you."

"IT WILL!" moaned Bertie. "Anyway, I can't go on Friday because ... Eugene's invited me for a sleepover at his house."

"You just made that up," said Mum. "Besides, it's all arranged now. You never know, you might actually enjoy it."

Enjoy it? thought Bertie, fat chance of that if Nick was going to be there.

Dirty Bertie

He slammed the front door and
stomped off down the road. Wait until
Darren and Eugene heard about this. At
least they'd understand.

"A sleepover – with Know-All Nick?"
giggled Darren. "HA HA! HEE HEE!"

Bertie folded his arms. His friends
seemed to think it was the best joke
they'd ever heard.

"It's not funny," he grumbled.

"It is pretty funny," said Darren.

"I wonder what you'll do all evening,"
said Eugene. "You could help Nick tidy
his bedroom."

"Or do your homework together,"
said Darren.

"It's too horrible for words," moaned
Bertie. "You've got to help me!"

"What can *we* do?" asked Eugene.
"I'm just amazed that Nick invited you."

"He didn't, that's the whole point!"
said Bertie. "It's all his mum's idea. He
probably hates it as much as I do…"

Bertie stopped dead. Wait a minute…

Dirty Bertie

Maybe it wasn't too late to get out
of it?

"I'll be right back," Bertie told his
friends. "I need to speak to Nick."

Know-All Nick was leaning against the
railings, waiting for the bell to go.

"Hello, Nick!" said Bertie.

"Huh, it's you," said Nick, with an icy
glare.

Bertie thought it was probably best to
get straight to the point.

"Look, you know this sleepover on
Friday!" he said. "I don't want to come."

"No kidding," sneered Nick. "Do you
think it was my idea? I wouldn't invite
you if you begged me on your knees."

"Well, I didn't," said Bertie. "It's bad
enough seeing you at school every day,
I don't want to see you at your house."

Dirty Bertie

"I can't think of anything worse!"
moaned Nick.

"For once we agree," said Bertie.
"Can't you get your mum to call it off?"

Nick shook his head. "I've tried," he
said. "I told her we're not friends. I said
you're smelly, you pick your nose and
you've got fleas – but she won't listen!
She says it's all arranged and it would be
rude to cancel."

"That's what my mum says too,"

sighed Bertie. "But there's got to be something we can do."

"There isn't," said Nick. "Trust me, if there was I'd have thought of it by now. We're stuck with it."

Bertie gave up. It was all their mums' fault, he thought bitterly. If they were so keen on the idea, why didn't they have their own sleepover?

CHAPTER 3

All too quickly, Friday arrived. Bertie
usually looked forward to Fridays as the
start of the weekend – no school, no
Miss Boot and no one shouting at him
to pay attention. Not this Friday though
– he had a whole evening of Know-All
Nick to endure.

At five o'clock Dad drove him over to

Dirty Bertie

Nick's house.

"Remember your manners," Dad said
as he rang the doorbell. "And please *try*
not to get into any trouble."

"When do I ever get in trouble?"
asked Bertie.

Dad gave him a look – it would take
too long to answer that question.

Mrs Wormsley opened the door.
"Ah, Bertie, here you are!" she clucked.
"Nicholas has been so looking forward
to this, haven't you, bunnikins?"

Bunnikins looked like he wanted to
crawl into a hole.

"Take Bertie's bag then, Nicholas, and
show him where to leave his shoes,"
said Mrs Wormsley.

Nick's house was modern and shiny,
like something in a magazine. Everything

Dirty Bertie

was spotlessly clean and smelled of polish. Bertie had to leave his shoes by the door. The lounge had a thick white carpet. The sofas and chairs were white leather. On every wall were photos of Know-All Nick: Nick in his school uniform, Nick on a sledge, Nick holding a skinny cat that was trying to escape.

Dirty Bertie

"The carpet's brand new," said Mrs Wormsley proudly. "That's why we don't wear our shoes indoors. We don't want to get it dirty, do we?"

Bertie glanced at his grubby hands and stuffed them in his pockets. It was probably best not to touch anything.

"Well, why don't you boys run along and play while I get supper ready?" said Nick's mum.

Upstairs Nick's bedroom was nothing like Bertie's room. The floor wasn't covered in socks, toys and half-eaten biscuits. Nick's shirts, ties and jackets hung neatly on a rail. His prizes and certificates hung on the wall, along with every school report.

Nicholas is such a joy to teach! If only his classmates were more like him.

Dirty Bertie

Nick flopped down on his bed.

"So what do you want to do then?" he asked sulkily.

Bertie shrugged. "I dunno. What do you normally do on a sleepover?"

"I don't have many sleepovers," said Nick. "Other children are so boring. I could show you my coin collection, I suppose."

"No thanks," said Bertie.

"I know, why don't we play schools!" suggested Nick. "I'll be the teacher and set you lots of homework."

"You must be kidding," said Bertie. "Can't we go outside? I'll be a pirate captain and take you prisoner."

"No way," said Nick. "I don't like rough games."

Bertie rolled his eyes. If Darren and Eugene were here, they'd be building their own den and raiding the kitchen for a midnight feast. Nick had probably never had a midnight feast in his life!

"This is boring!" grumbled Nick. "I wish you'd just go home."

"Me too," said Bertie.

Nick lay back on his pillow, thinking. Suddenly he shot upright with an idea.

"Listen, there's only one way you could go home – if my parents sent you," he said.

Bertie frowned. "Why would they do that?"

Nick smiled. "If you did something really, really bad."

"Oh, yeah, that's all right for you," said Bertie. "I'll be the one who gets in trouble."

Nick shrugged. "I'm never in trouble, I'm just no good at it," he said. "But you're always in trouble so it shouldn't be difficult. Anyway, don't you want to go home?"

Bertie considered it. It would mean joining forces with Nick, which was normally out of the question. But this was an emergency and it would put

an end to the world's worst sleepover.
He could be home eating pizza and
watching TV, while Nick could go back
to counting his coin collection.

"It's up to you," said Nick. "Or we
can just stay here and I'll show you my
certificates."

That settled it.

"Okay, I'm in," said Bertie. "What do
I have to do?"

CHAPTER 4

At six o'clock they sat down to supper.
Nick's mum had made watery vegetable
soup. Nick and his parents took dainty
sips from their spoons. Bertie glanced
at Nick who gave him a nod. Time for
"Operation Home Time". Bertie raised
his soup bowl to his lips.

"SHLUUUURPP!"

"Goodness!" cried Nick's mum. "Where are your manners, Bertie?"

"Sorry, that's how we eat soup at home," explained Bertie.

"Good heavens!" said Nick's dad. "Use your spoon, that's what it's for!"

Bertie picked up his spoon and shovelled soup into his mouth. Then he sat back, patted his stomach and gave a long, loud…

"BURRRRRRRRP!"

It was one of his best, an absolute ripper. Nick's dad almost fell off his chair.

"REALLY!" he said. "I hope you don't do that at home?"

"Oh yes," replied Bertie. "Our family always has burping contests at the table. If you think I'm loud you should hear my mum!"

Dirty Bertie

Nick's mum and dad exchanged worried looks. The boy had no manners at all and his family sounded revolting.

Dessert was served. Bertie talked with his mouth full and wiped his nose on the tablecloth. He spilled trifle on his jumper and licked it off. Nick's mum tutted loudly while his dad looked like he might explode. Nevertheless Bertie was their guest and they pretended not to mind.

Dirty Bertie

After supper Bertie and Nick went
back upstairs.

"It's not working," said Nick. "You
need to try harder."

"I'm doing my best!" grumbled Bertie.
"It's not easy being disgusting!"

He slumped on Nick's bed – it wasn't
even seven o'clock. Unless he thought of
something they had hours of boredom
ahead. He looked out of the window. It
had started to rain.

Bertie smiled. "You know I suggested
playing pirates? How about we play
outside?"

"Don't be stupid," said Nick. "We'd
get soaking wet."

"Exactly. Wet *and* muddy," agreed
Bertie. "And the thing about pirates is,
they never take their boots off."

Dirty Bertie

Nick's eyes grew bigger. If Bertie meant what he thought, it would cause a riot.

"WE CAN'T!" he wailed. "My mum will go up the wall!"

"Probably," smiled Bertie. "You'll be sent to bed and I'll be sent home."

Dirty Bertie

Nick's parents were clearing up in the kitchen. Mr Wormsley closed the dishwasher.

"What's that horrible noise?" he asked.

They listened. Loud whoops and shrieks of excitement reached their ears. It sounded like it was coming from the garden.

"The boys are upstairs, aren't they?" asked Nick's mum.

She opened the back door and gasped. Bertie and her son were chasing each other round the garden. Their clothes were soaked and their shoes were caked in mud. A horrible thought crossed her mind. Stepping out, she saw that the French doors were wide open.

Dirty Bertie

Surely not?

She rushed back into the lounge.

"NOOOO!" she screamed. "MY BEAUTIFUL NEW CARPET!"

Dirty Bertie

A trail of footprints made a muddy pattern across the white carpet. Splodgy marks on the white sofa and chairs suggested pirates had been bouncing on them.

"NICHOLAS! BERTIE!" screeched Mrs Wormsley. "GET IN HERE RIGHT NOW!"

Things moved fairly quickly after that. Mr Wormsley phoned Bertie's parents to come and collect him. Nick was packed off to bed. As he went upstairs he glanced back at Bertie with a sly smile.

Bertie nodded to him.

During the drive home Bertie's dad kept a stony silence.

"Oh well," sighed Bertie. "I guess I won't be invited round for any more sleepovers."

Dirty Bertie

"No, I very much doubt it," said Dad through gritted teeth.

Bertie sat back and yawned happily. For a moment then, he'd almost enjoyed playing pirates in the rain. It wouldn't last, of course. On Monday, Nick would be back to his old smug self and the two of them would be at war again. Bertie couldn't wait.

CHAPTER 1

Bertie and his friends were playing cricket on the field before school.

TWHACK! Darren's bat cracked the ball.

"Catch it, Bertie!" cried Eugene.

Bertie looked up as the tennis ball rocketed towards him. At the last minute he ducked. The ball bounced once on the grass and ran away across the playground.

"Six!" cried Darren. "That's thirty-two not out."

Bertie pulled a face.

"Go on then, get it," said Darren.

Bertie trudged off. He couldn't see the point of cricket. Most of the time it involved fetching the ball so that Darren could wallop it somewhere else.

The ball had rolled to a stop at someone's feet. "Oh no," groaned Bertie. The feet belonged to Masher Martin, the biggest bully in the school!

Masher was in the top year. Next to Bertie and his friends, he looked like a giant – the kind that ate small children.

Masher bent down and picked up the ball.

"What's the problem?" asked Darren.

Bertie pointed.

"Oh no, not Masher Martin!" moaned Eugene.

"Just ask him to give the ball back," said Darren.

"YOU ask him," said Bertie.

"I'm batting, you're the fielder," argued Darren.

Bertie sighed.

"Why's it always left to me?" he muttered as he headed towards Masher.

Dirty Bertie

He'd heard all the stories. Masher
had his own seat on the school bus
and always pushed in to be first in
the dinner queue. Once he'd dumped
Trevor in a wheelie bin just for "staring
at him". Even Mr Weakly was scared of
Masher and he was a teacher!

"Hi, Masher," squeaked Bertie.
"Actually, that's our ball."

Masher stared at him
as if he was a small
insect.

Dirty Bertie

Bertie tried again.

"So anyway, could we have it back?"

Masher folded his arms. "Ask me nicely," he grunted.

Bertie glanced back at his friends. He knew this was a bad idea.

"Please, Masher, can we have our ball back?" he sighed.

Masher shrugged and held the tennis ball out to him. The moment Bertie reached for it, he snatched it away.

"HAR! HAR!" he hooted. "You know what? I think I'll keep it. Unless you want to argue?"

"ME?" said Bertie.

"Yeah YOU, maggot," growled Masher, leaning in close. Bertie did the only sensible thing – he turned and ran.

"Where's the ball?" asked Darren.

Dirty Bertie

"He won't give it back," Bertie panted.

"But it's our ball, he can't just steal it!" cried Darren.

"Who's stealing?" whined a voice behind them.

Bertie swung round. Trust Know-All Nick to be earwigging on their conversation.

"Masher Martin's got our ball," explained Eugene. "Bertie asked but he won't give it back."

"Bertie? HA! HA!" jeered Nick. "I bet he was too scared to speak."

"I was not!" said Bertie. "Masher Martin doesn't scare me."

"Oh no?" said Nick.

"No," said Bertie. "He's just a big, ugly bully and one of these days I'll teach him a lesson."

Dirty Bertie

The words were out
before he could stop
them. Nick looked
delighted.

"Well, I'm sure
Masher would be very
interested to hear
that!" he smirked.

Bertie stared. "No, wait … you're not
actually going to tell him?"

"Why not?" said Nick. "You wanted
to teach him a lesson, well this could be
your big chance!"

He patted Bertie on the back and
walked off, wearing a huge grin.

"Uh-oh. Now you've done it!" said
Darren.

"What did you say that for?" asked
Eugene.

Dirty Bertie

"He's bluffing," said Bertie. "He wouldn't really tell Masher, would he?"

"I wouldn't put it past him," said Eugene. "And then you're *really* in big trouble."

CHAPTER 2

All that morning Bertie found it impossible to concentrate. Miss Boot droned on about commas and full stops but he didn't hear a word. He kept expecting to see Masher's big, ugly face at the door. He couldn't remember exactly what he'd said but the words "teach him a lesson" stuck in his mind.

Dirty Bertie

What on earth made him say it? Couldn't he keep his big mouth shut for once? If Masher ever found out, he was toast. His only chance was to lie low and keep out of sight.

At break time, Bertie hid behind Darren and Eugene.

"What are you playing at?" asked Darren.

"I don't want to run into Masher," said Bertie. "Can you see him?"

Darren looked around the playground.

"He's over there talking to someone," he said.

"Not just someone, it's Know-All Nick," said Eugene.

"You're kidding!" groaned Bertie. "What are they saying?"

"How should we know?" said Darren.

Dirty Bertie

"Watch out, they're coming over!"

Bertie panicked. He had to hide and quickly! He dived behind a bench and lay flat on his belly, his heart pounding. Darren and Eugene sat down to try and hide him. Seconds later, footsteps approached.

Dirty Bertie

"Where's Bertie?" whined Nick.

"Yeah, where's the maggot?" grunted Masher.

"We haven't seen him," lied Darren.

"No, I think he probably went home," said Eugene.

Nick narrowed his eyes.

"Liars!" he said.

Getting down on all fours, he peered under the bench.

"Oh, there you are, Bertie!" he crowed. "Hiding away like a little mouse!"

Bertie crawled out. "I was ... just looking for my hanky," he explained.

Nick pointed.

"That's him," he said. "He's the one I told you about."

"I didn't!" said Bertie.

"Didn't what?" growled Masher.

Dirty Bertie

"I didn't call you 'a big, ugly bully'," said Bertie.

"Told you," said Nick. "And that's not all. He's going to teach you a lesson, isn't that right, Bertie?"

"NO!" wailed Bertie. "I was talking about someone else!"

Masher grabbed him by his shirt, lifting him clean off the ground.

"You and me, on the field after school," he said. "Got it, maggot?"

"Yes, got it!" croaked Bertie.

Masher set him down.

"Be there or I'll come looking," he snarled. "Don't forget!"

Dirty Bertie

He stomped away, clearing a wide
path through the other children.

"What's he mean: 'Me and him on
the field'? Are we playing cricket?" asked
Bertie.

"Don't be stupid," sneered Nick.
"He's going to fight you."

"FIGHT ME?" gasped Bertie, his voice
rising in panic.

A fight with
Masher Martin, the
biggest bully in the
school? He
was going to
need a suit of
armour.

CHAPTER 3

After break, they had Art. Bertie perched on a stool while Darren and Eugene painted splodgy portraits of him.

"Keep still. Don't talk and don't fidget," boomed Miss Boot.

But Bertie couldn't keep still. He jiggled his legs nervously. All he could think about was facing Masher after school. He'd never fought anyone in his life. What was the point of fighting anyway? Someone always got hurt and in this case it would be him!

"Sit still!" grumbled Darren.

"I CAN'T!" moaned Bertie. "Listen, why don't we all fight him? With three of us we'd stand a chance."

"No fear, he's massive!" said Eugene. "Anyway, my mum doesn't like me fighting."

"Size isn't everything," said Darren. "You could try judo on him."

"I don't know any judo," moaned Bertie.

"Neither do I," said Darren. "But I've seen it on the telly."

"You know what you should do? Tell a teacher," said Eugene. "Tell Miss Boot."

Dirty Bertie

"You think she'd listen?" asked Bertie.

"BERTIE! What did I just say?" barked Miss Boot. "Stop talking!"

Bertie decided he was in enough trouble already. What if Masher found out he'd gone running to a teacher? If only he could leave school before the bell went! Actually, that wasn't a bad idea…

His eyes fell on the tube of red paint Darren was using. That might do the trick. When no one was looking, he squeezed a blob on to his finger and hid the tube in his pocket. Now to get Miss Boot's attention.

"ARGHH! OWW!" he howled.

"What's the matter, Bertie?" groaned Miss Boot.

"I've cut my finger! It's bleeding!" cried Bertie.

Dirty Bertie

Miss Boot marched over. She seized
Bertie's finger to examine it.

"Do I need to go to
hospital?" asked Bertie
hopefully.

"I doubt it, that's
red paint," snapped
Miss Boot. "Do you
think I was born
yesterday?"

"Nice try, Bertie,"
grinned Darren.

Bertie shook his
head. There was no
escape. At home time
Masher Martin would be waiting
for him on the field. At least the fight
would be over quickly. He'd probably
pass out before they started.

CHAPTER 4

Bertie watched the clock hands creep closer to home time. Maybe Masher Martin wouldn't turn up? Maybe he'd done enough bullying for one day? The bell rang and Bertie jumped out of his skin.

He trailed out of school with Darren and Eugene. A small crowd had gathered on the field. Know-All Nick was there – obviously he'd spread the word about the fight of the century: Masher Martin v Wimpy Bertie.

"OH, BERTIE! Over here!" sang Nick. "We're all waiting for you!"

Bertie's heart sank.

"It's no good," said Darren. "You'll just have to stand up to him."

"It's not too late," said Eugene. "I could still find a teacher."

Bertie wished he'd listened earlier. Right now he would have been relieved to see Miss Boot or even Mr Weakly. Where were all the teachers when you needed one?

Dirty Bertie

It was too late now because Masher Martin had arrived.

"Right then, maggot," he growled. "Let's get started."

Bertie felt his legs turn to jelly.

"Remember, keep moving," Darren whispered. "Tire him out then hit him with the judo moves I showed you."

The crowd had formed a rough circle with Bertie in the middle. He looked round. Darren gave him a thumbs up but Eugene had vanished. *So much for friends!* thought Bertie.

"What's the matter? Not trying to chicken out, Bertie?" jeered Nick.

Masher lumbered forward. Bertie took Darren's advice and danced out of reach. They circled round to the left, then back to the right.

Dirty Bertie

"Keep still!" growled Masher. "You're making me dizzy."

Suddenly he made a grab for Bertie. Bertie dodged out of reach and crawled through his legs. Masher whirled round, but Bertie wasn't there. He'd jumped on Masher's back and was clinging on for dear life.

"GET OFF ME!" roared Masher.

1

Dirty Bertie

He twisted this way and that, trying to shake Bertie loose. But Bertie hung on tight, knowing he was safer where he was. The crowd started cheering. No one liked the school bully so they were all supporting Bertie.

"Hang on, Bertie! You're on top!" shouted Darren.

This was sort of true but not for long. The next moment Masher swung round and Bertie lost his grip. He was thrown off, landing on the grass with a thump. Something in his pocket squelched. Bertie looked up and saw Masher's big, ugly face grinning down at him. So this was it – curtains – he was a goner.

Suddenly Masher gaped, his eyes wide with panic.

"W-what's that?" he gasped, pointing.

"It's not blood?"

Bertie looked down at his jeans.
A large red patch had spread from his
pocket. It certainly looked like blood…

"ARGHH! URGHH!" moaned Bertie,
clutching his side.

"Now you've done it," said Darren.
"Better call an ambulance."

Masher had turned very pale.

"But … I didn't touch him! It wasn't
my fault!" he wailed.

"Try telling that to Miss Boot," said
Darren. "Here she comes!"

Bertie sneaked a look. Miss Boot was
striding furiously towards them with
Eugene at her side. Masher didn't wait
to explain. He fled across the field with
a wail of terror.

"HEEEEELP!"

"What's going on?" thundered Miss Boot. "I will NOT have fighting in school!"

"I wasn't fighting!" said Bertie. "He was fighting me!"

"Telltale!" muttered Nick.

"QUIET, Nicholas!" snapped Miss Boot. "I'm surprised at you. From what I hear you're the one who started all this."

Dirty Bertie

Nick turned crimson.

"Well, Bertie, are you actually hurt?" asked Miss Boot, holding out a hand.

Bertie got to his feet.

"Not really. I'm feeling much better now," he said.

Miss Boot folded her arms. "Next time someone tries to bully you, come and tell me right away," she said. "Do you understand?"

Bertie nodded.

"I will deal with Mr Martin in the morning. And you too, Nicholas," said Miss Boot. She glanced at Bertie's red stained jeans. "As for you, Bertie, if that's what I think it is, you better get those jeans in the wash."

"Yes, Miss Boot," mumbled Bertie. "And, um, thanks."

Dirty Bertie

They headed out of the gate and turned for home. Bertie could hardly believe his luck. For once Miss Boot hadn't shouted at him ... in fact she'd actually taken his side! He doubted if Masher Martin or Nick would get off so lightly tomorrow morning. He noticed Eugene staring at him.

"That stuff on your jeans – it's not blood at all, is it?" said Eugene.

"Of course not!" laughed Darren.

Bertie put his hand in his pocket and produced a messy tube of red paint.

"I forgot this was in my pocket," he said. "I guess it must have burst open when I landed on the grass."

Eugene grinned. "Trust you, Bertie!"

"Well, it certainly fooled Masher," said Darren. "You should have seen his face when I said Miss Boot was coming!"

"Serves him right for being such a big bully," said Bertie. "I told you."

"Told us what?" asked Eugene.

"I told you I'd teach him a lesson one day!"